RECKLESSLY ABANDONED

(A TRUE STORY)

Published by:

OUT OF AFRICA PUBLISHING
P.O. Box 34685
Kansas City, MO 64116
U.S.A.

(816) 734-0493
shekmin@aol.com
Web site: www.kalibu.com

All scriptures quoted are out of the King James Version of the Bible unless otherwise notated.

Copyright © 1996
Michael Howard

All rights reserved. No part of this book may be reproduced in any form, except for the inclusion of brief quotations, without prior permission in writing from the author.

Printed in the United States of America.
3rd Edition 2001

ISBN: 1-888529-00-8

TABLE OF CONTENTS

1. THE ENEMY 9
2. THE ENCOUNTER 17
3. DEATH'S JAW 31
4. AMNESTY 49
5. SCHOOL 59
6. ELIM: LORD WE DON'T UNDERSTAND 69
7. BACK TO THE BUSH 75
8. REVIVAL 89
9. UTTERMOST 103
10. CRY BELOVED LAND 113
11. MISSION IMPOSSIBLE 127
12. BLOOD OF THE MARTYRS 151
13. NEW BEGINNINGS 167

DEDICATION

To **HIM** for whom I live and am also ready to die: my beloved Lord Jesus Christ who gave His all for me and inspired my life.

Be glorified through this book, Lord!

MICHAEL HOWARD

CHAPTER ONE

THE ENEMY

The moon shone brightly, her light filtering through the motionless trees of the pine forest while the stars twinkled like myriads of jewels on a purple velvet cloth. It was cold, bitterly cold, in those eastern mountains on that typically clear African winter night. In fact, it was so cold that everything was stilled: the breezes, the insects, and the owls. There would be frost that night.

"O Lord, please don't let anyone's teeth start chattering. And please don't let a snake, scorpion or spider become anyone's bed partner," Jonathan whispered. Jonathan himself had had that experience when a deadly cobra had eased itself into his sleeping bag one night to share some of his body warmth. Fortunately the vile creature had become entangled in the blanket lining giving Jonathan the chance of a speedy exit. He then crushed the serpent's head with his boot. Only the bitter cold had driven him back into the sleeping bag but this time he zipped and tied in tight. He shuddered as he thought of it. Under normal circumstances he would have yelled but those were not normal circumstances and nor were these! Caution was absolutely essential now.

Peter, just a kid of eighteen and straight out of school, lay two arms-length below Jonathan along the descending mountain path. It was Peter's first sortie and Jonathan could feel the ground vibrating from Peter's fearful heartthrob. He was scared, petrified in fact. This was the real thing. All the training, the tactics, the weapons drill could never adequately prepare one for the first real encounter. Jonathan reached out his hand to Peter whose arm shot out in response. Grabbing his hand, Jonathan gave a reassuring squeeze as he remembered Peter quietly but somewhat frantically asking him earlier, "Sir, will I die tonight?"

"Of course not, kid," Jonathan had emphatically said as way of encouragement but knowing that it was only God who could protect. A stray bullet, a sniper, an ambush, a land mine, only God's Spirit had kept the Bible Jonathan and his armor bearer from the Philistines, and only God's Spirit can really keep us from death,

Jonathan had reasoned in his mind before explaining to Peter the wonderful story of redemption and the security of the Lord.

"That explains, Sir, why all your black soldiers talk about you the way they do and always want to be with you. They've told me. They really honor you and treat you like a hero. They've told me of your escapes..."

"They're very superstitious. Yes, it's only the Lord, Peter. Without Him I can really do nothing. You do need to know Him," Jonathan urged. It's a wonderfully exciting and secure life walking with Jesus. Think about it."

As Jonathan released Peter's hand the kid whispered, "I've thought about it, Sir. I do want Jesus..." Though excited, Jonathan motioned absolute silence in the moonlight. A whisper could really carry in the stillness and the enemy had fine-tuned ears. It was their life. They were like the animals of the jungle: their five senses were highly sharpened.

Jonathan rehearsed the procedure in his mind. Was there anything he'd forgotten to tell his men? They were strung out along the mountain path, buried under pine needles and leaves. Faces, arms, hair, had all been daubed with blacking. No watches, chains or even medic alerts were to be worn with the possibility of them shining in the moonlight. The stops had been positioned well ahead and behind the rest of the group. The men had been cautioned not to fire on the "mujibas". These were young teenage boys who had been taken from herding the cattle and goats to become the messengers and spies for the enemy. They were also forced to run ahead of the enemy so that if there were an ambush they would take all the flack or if there were anti-personnel mines the mujibas would detonate them leaving the enemy unscathed. This was real war: kill or be killed, do or die!

Jonathan had chosen a classic ambush position. The section of path was an elongated "S" with a sheer precipice on the side opposite where they lay. Once trapped in the "S" the enemy would be brought down. Vengeance was in the air - information received by Jonathan told that this was part of the marauding gang that had done so much damage and inflicted so much torture and death on the local villagers. It was time they were stopped...

Suddenly the alarm of a breaking twig in the silence announced the enemy without any other warning. A soft patter of bare feet and the first mujibas had passed. Then, there were some more. Those native boys were naked to their waist, their sinewy chests and arms shining in the moonlight. They were very close. Jonathan eased off the safety catch of his automatic FN rifle. He had twenty rounds in the magazine and three more full magazines. The adrenaline was pumping fast now as he heard the "clack", "clack" sound of one of the enemy's ammunition belts banging against the butt of his RPG 7 machine gun. "Good," thought Jonathan, "he won't even have time to get it off his shoulder..." Before he even finished his thought the first of the enemy came around the bend right into his sights. He was a short, stocky fellow and was followed quickly by four others. A brief gap then...there he was...the real enemy...all six feet and more of him. Thin and sinewy like the mujibas he wore his wiry hair in plaits around the edges but wildly Afro on top. He walked with that characteristic sway of a tall man who doesn't know what to do with his long legs. He was dressed in the green fatigues of the East Germans and decked with badges, crests, necklaces and bangles - no doubt the spoils of those he had massacred. So this was the notorious "Kufa Ufulu" (the spirit of death) at close range. His very name struck fear and dread into the natives and it seemed he was invincible. Jonathan had seen him before through binoculars but he had eluded every move to trap him, ambush him or capture him. There was a strange power about him: it was almost tangible, almost like an evil mantra protecting him.

"That's it," Jonathan almost shouted, "He's full of devils! He's a devil doing the devil's work - nobody can be that naturally evil looking and do the evil deeds he does...."

Suddenly it was supernatural power versus supernatural power in a very natural war. The hunter tonight had become the hunted and was within Jonathan's grasp. The adrenaline pumped even harder sending shivers down his back while his mouth was dry with tenseness and excitement. This was rather routine compared to some of what Jonathan had experienced but here was the real enemy, the devil himself incarnate in Kufa Ufulu that "spirit of death."

All these observations and thoughts flashed through Jonathan's mind in a second. It is amazing how pressure can stimulate the thought process. In a flash Kufa Ufulu was already a silhouette down the path but his image was indelibly imprinted on Jonathan's retina. Somehow, somewhere, sometime they would meet face to face. Jonathan knew it deep inside. The Spirit inside him surged to confront this enemy who had wrecked havoc in multitudes of lives. This was the real terrorist of the terrible Rhodesian (now Zimbabwe) war which strung out over fourteen years from 1967 to 1980 and Jonathan was right in the midst of it.

It was then split second timing. A dozen "terrs" (colloquial term for terrorist) had already passed Jonathan's position and more were coming. The lead terr would be about mid-way into the ambush. Jonathan silently prayed that everyone would hold his fire. The signal for action to commence was for the front stop to open up with his machine gun but what if this gang was fifty or a hundred strong? Seconds that seemed like hours passed - Jonathan lost count at twenty and more were still coming!

Shattering the still cold night, the noise exploded and echoed back from mountaintop to mountaintop as if a thousand bombs were falling. In that split second Jonathan pressed his trigger. All he could hear was the crack of his own rifle and the smell of spent gunpowder. A continuous line of flashes emerged from below the path and Jonathan could see tracer bullets whiz through the air. Some exploded on distant rocks, others tore trees to shreds while still others found their mark on human flesh. A terr leaped into the air over where Jonathan lay only to catch a bullet and fall like lead in mid-flight crumpling dead against the foot of a tree. Others were rolling off the path and some had dived off the precipice.

There was chaos. Terrs were falling, running, screaming: Dismay and unbelief; fear and agony was etched upon faces shining in the moonlight. They were very close to the men. This couldn't be happening to them! Why hadn't the mujibas done their job? Why no warning? Pine trees were no protection from red-hot tracer cutting through them like wire through a cheese. Nothing could be heard but cracking rifles and ringing ears but the eyes saw and told the whole truth. Jonathan kept wondering if Ufulu had been hit, but... and it was a big "BUT" for he knew his men and doubted. If his own spiritual life inspired them, Jonathan also knew that the witchcraft, the "medicine," the drugs and drink which saturated Kufa Ufulu would send fear waves rippling through them. Of his twenty-four men that night, four only were white, the rest were black and very prone to superstition. They believed in the ancestral spirits, they believed they could be "smelled out;" they believed in appeasement and they were ruled by fear as Africa is even in the twentieth century.

Every terr at initiation had made a blood covenant to Mbuya Nehanda. Mbuya means "the revered mother" and she had been a famous witch much like Gagool in the epic "King Solomon's Mines." She had ruled Southern Rhodesia through fear and intimidation and had incited the Shona tribe to a great rebellion against the British in 1897. She was hanged for her role but before dying, promised that her spirit would live on and return to lead the natives to victory against the whites. Her wickedness and power had known no limitations and now she was the great and unseen spirit who had taken effective leadership of the terrorist armies.

Making covenant to her was practiced in various ways but usually entailed killing and drinking the blood of an heroic animal such as a lion, elephant, buffalo, rhinoceros or even the aggressive black mamba snake. Then, the terrorist began to take on the nature and characteristics of that creature. During his first battle, the partly initiated terr must get the blood of his first kill, mix it with his own, offer some to Mbuya and drink the rest. For her part, Mbuya repaid with strength and power, invincibility and invisibility in battle. So much the better if the terr could drink a white man's blood - he was promised total power over them and their bullets would never harm him.

The most frightening experience of the war was to see terrs pumped full of lead but still, they kept on coming. It seemed nothing could stop them because they were so full of evil spirits. This often caused great alarm and fear in the natives of the Rhodesian forces who had no understanding of the power of the mind, physiology or the pure workings of demonic control.

That night Jonathan knew there was the real probability that none of his men would dare to shoot at Ufulu. He was already a legend and nobody was going to risk killing him only to have Ufulu's spirit haunt him and torment him to death.

"This is a double battle we're fighting," sighed Jonathan, "how shall we ever win against such trends? It's pure wickedness. To fight in the natural is one thing but this is supernatural and our own forces don't even understand it. It's a losing battle. No wonder Paul says we wrestle against spiritual wickedness in high places."

Deep down, Jonathan knew he was right. Kufa Ufulu would escape because of the fear and superstition of Africa and the very real powers of darkness that overrode military orders. There was always hope though.

Without anyone motioning, the firing instantly ceased. Nobody moved, spoke or made the slightest noise. The orders had been clear and strict. Everybody was to maintain his place until daylight. Some terrs might feign death, they might regroup and return - not likely but possible - and one of his own men might be accidentally shot, being mistaken for the enemy.

The African bush had returned to silence only this time an eerie kind. Everybody's hair was standing up on his neck and this was the time when the eyes played tricks. Stare at a tree for a few seconds too long and it soon appeared as if it had grown arms and legs. Look away and blink...then the tree had moved...then it had an AK 47 assault rifle and coming towards you.... The imagination ran riot at times like that and the strictest discipline was required not to shoot. Every man was to have immediately changed from automatic to repeat fire. After about thirty minutes of stillness and frozen calm, there was a sudden rush as three terrs fled up the path. Instantly, half a dozen rifles cracked. Two of the terrs crumpled and the third escaped...NOT for long...Jim, the backstop was alert. A short burst of machine gun fire told the story. There were a few groans from the injured but nobody dared to move and there was still two hours until sun up.

Peter's teeth began to chatter uncontrollably. Poor kid. At least he had come through though. Jonathan rolled over whispering, "bury yourself in your sleeping bag and chew on your blanket. Make sure your safety catch is fast and your rifle is ready. I think it's over now but we must always be alert." It was not long after the kid disappeared into his bag that he soon fell sound asleep. Jonathan smiled. He called Peter "Kid" but he himself was only four years Peter's senior. The difference though was that Jonathan had already graduated from University at nineteen, taught for a year and traveled.

The rest of the night passed uneventfully except for a heavy frost which covered everything in a thin layer of ice. It was bitterly cold for a warm-blooded African. Jonathan wished he were in his little cottage under four warm blankets instead of out there.... But, no thoughts could dispel the uppermost nagging: did they get Kufa Ufulu? He couldn't have escaped. Jonathan patiently, though anxiously waited through the changing colors of the dawn from deep purple to pale pink, then orange followed by flaming yellow.

"How beautiful your handiwork, Lord!" he whispered, "even in the midst of all this."

It was at that time that he gave the signal to his sergeant. Taking five men, Sergeant Khami made his way under cover and with back up support up the hill towards the end stop who had already been signaled. The injured were carefully examined to be sure they were not lying on a live grenade. Finally, the "all clear" was given and while the men emerged from the undergrowth Corporal Kizito radioed for the helicopters to come in.

Jonathan posted his men and then began to survey the damage. Bodies lay strewn along the mountain path: that one's face was blown away; another had lost his arm while his comrade had a hole in the stomach. Another had died in torment and pain, which was registered upon his face, but there was no sign of Kufa Ufulu; the "spirit of death" had vanished.

"I can't believe it," shouted Jonathan, "the devil does take care of his own - he's eluded us again."

As Jonathan looked at the dead, the injured, his men, the African dawn, he spoke audibly to himself, "This is a bloody, bloody, war. What am I doing here?" His mind began to wonder back to the stream of events that had brought him to this point starting with his conversion as a young boy of twelve and an immediate thirst to do something for the Lord.

CHAPTER TWO

THE ENCOUNTER

Jonathan had grown up during the last days of really wild Africa: you know, when the elephants grazed on the front lawn in the early morning and the lions came to the back door to give you a wake up growl. His Dad was in the famous British South Africa Police at a time when constables went out on three - month patrols, horseback being the only mode of transport. His Mom was left at the station to oversee affairs including supervising the prisoners (called bandits). But then, that was when a local native was told to walk three weeks to report to "the madame - Nkosikazi" who would put him in prison for some misdemeanor. They never failed to go and never failed to report, "Nkosi (the big boss) `says lock me up'."
That Africa was the legacy of those noble missionaries: David Livingstone and Robert Moffat and the great white hunter, Selous; the Africa where "colonialism" was not yet a bad word and white men were not hated and seen only as exploiters; days when one was blessed if one possessed a paraffin (kerosene) fridge, when one lived by the light of tilly lanterns and the old cast iron wood stove. What meals they could produce. That was the Africa when Jonathan at age six and his younger brother could be safely entrusted to a couple of "bandits" and be gone for days exploring the forests and vast uninhabited bushveld. How well he remembered his favorite bandit who had served his time and was to be freed. Dick had said, "Nkosikazi, I'll be back next week to take care of the picannini (young) nkosis." Sure enough a week later he was back. He'd deliberately broken into a store so that he would be arrested again in order to continue looking after the picannini Nkosis.
That was noble Africa, honorable Africa before the "winds of change" brought guns, westernization and materialism to a Continent which was not ready to handle it. That was the "Dark Continent" emerging into infancy before becoming a pawn in the cold war of communism and being plunged back into darkness; the Africa before tarred highways, electricity, jet airplanes and fast

cars. The first family car Jonathan remembered was an old 1938 hump - back Ford. It was made of solid steel and the back window was so high his Mom couldn't see out to reverse. The kids had to stand on the back seat and shout - inevitably they were too late: reversing procedure usually ended by hitting a tree, a fence post, a garden wall but there was never a dent on the old Crock. Later she was sold to a native pig farmer who "taxied" his pigs to town in her. At last count, he had rolled her three times but she was still going strong....

It was in that environment that fishing, hunting and tracking were more important than school. It was in that vast paradise of God's creation that Jonathan became acutely aware of the Master's handiwork and an unslaked thirst began to grow in him for reality; a questioning from the earliest age of who he was, from where did he come and what was the purpose of life? Perhaps it was that Jonathan had always been a sickly child. Operated on ten days from birth for a pyloric stenosis - the only anesthetic being a teaspoon of brandy in those days - he often teetered on the borders of death. After a somewhat checkered recovery he went home to the most remote outpost of Mphoengs - a small house and three tin huts for an office - on the Bechaunaland (now Botswana) border. It was the terrible floods of the mid 1950's when every outpost was cut off from civilization and everyone had to live according to his wits and what he could shoot to eat. The smallest watercourses were turned into swollen rivers while rivers became raging torrents of red mud. It seemed as if the whole world was swept along in them -trees, wild animals, cattle, even vehicles. The only food was game meat - roasted, stewed, braaied (barbecue) boiled, dried - and that was scarce. The rains continued for months and milk formula soon ran out. There was no flying doctor service, no helicopters and no rural ambulance system. But, there was one brave native policeman who swam the swollen waters of the mighty Shashi River and walked thirty miles to Francistown to buy milk and meat. He swam back across the river with the meat in a plate clenched between his teeth - all for a white baby and his elder sister whom he loved. That is real heroism.

Somehow - it was God - Jonathan survived just as he survived asthma, the chicken pox and measles, the injuries, the epilepsy, all of which plagued his growing years. And, as he grew, he was thirsty, thirsty, thirsty. Thirsty for Reality whatever it was. Church was a bore - though the family seldom went - and the only recollection of Sunday School was telling the teacher that his father gave his mother a regular Friday night beating to keep her in order. This brought an immediate visit of a most concerned Sunday school teacher who was reassured that it was only a teaser. But in all this was the unseen directing hand of an Almighty God, infinitely concerned with one person, with one ordinary family.

Some weeks before his thirteenth birthday, having just witnessed a remarkable change in his elder sister who had "gotten saved and gone religious," Jonathan entered his bedroom one afternoon. Sitting down on the bed - no formula, no religious posture, no prayers - Jonathan said simply, forthrightly, "God, if you're real, I really want to know you." What transpired both startled him and filled him with awe. Suddenly, the room began to fill with bright light, so bright that it was white. The light was as real as to be almost tangible. Aghast, but not afraid, Jonathan opened his mouth in amazement. It was awesome. As he sat transfixed with mouth agape, the light moved towards him like a swirling mist. It entered his open mouth and descended into his deepest belly. He felt the warmth of it as it went down. When it had settled in his belly he felt a peace and joy he'd never known before... and more, much more than anything, he knew that he knew JESUS. Jesus is God and He had come in response to a young boy's sincere cry. There had been no church, no preacher, no Bible; only the cry of a lost soul searching for TRUTH and the TRUTH had revealed Himself. What a God! What a salvation!

The elation which Jonathan felt was indescribable; there was no compulsion to run and tell it abroad: the boy merely pondered it in his heart. A few days later, in a simple but equally sincere way, Jonathan sat on the same bed and said, "God, I'll serve you the rest of my life. I'm yours. I'll be a missionary for you." Jonathan didn't even know what a missionary was: the only type he had ever heard of were the political trouble shooters who were always inciting their followers to disobey the Government and break the law. A missionary - oh how his Dad despised them and always spoke disparagingly about them and here he was committing himself to being one.

It was some weeks before Jonathan confided in his sister, "I've given my heart to Jesus." Big sister was thrilled and it was not long before their young brother joined the other two. They attended a local Baptist church. At the end of a baptismal service one Sunday evening, the Pastor challenged others who felt the call to be baptized. As the organ played "I Surrender All..." Jonathan felt a supernatural power lift him to his feet. Before he knew it, he was at the front kneeling and praying. How he got there he doesn't remember to this day, but what joy to find brother and sister also in the line. The three were baptized together a few months later. Mom and Dad could not understand the fuss nor see any need for "being saved." The only thing they did see was that the kids no longer wanted to go fishing on Sundays but preferred to go to church - and twice at that! "Oh, it's a teenage fad and will pass," his mom said.

"Why don't you take your...beds to church and live there..." Dad had shouted. Jonathan had made the cardinal mistake of saying one night at supper, "Well, Dad, you should be honored. The whole church is praying for you..." That's as far as it got. With his characteristic parade ground voice and fists hitting the table simultaneously so that every plate, glass, dish and spoon rose off the table quivering, Jonathan's dad protested vehemently that he didn't need the...prayers or their... salvation. He was "off in the morning to tell the pastor so." It was the devil protesting. It would take twenty-two years of prayers and struggles before that military man finally "came through."

They were glorious and exciting years of growth and service for the Lord despite the changing face of Rhodesia and Africa at large. In the midst of Jonathan's high school years, the communist - backed terrorist insurgency began. At the same time, a significant visitor arrived at the Baptist church, one who was to make a profound impact on Jonathan and stir him for his first missionary service, though Jonathan had already felt a deep call to China.

Into his life walked Richard Wurmbrand of the Christian Mission to the Communist World and his famous book, Tortured for Christ. The young man and the old warrior were immediately united in spirit as Richard and his jewel of a wife, Sabina, shared of the plight of thousands, if not millions, of Christians behind the Iron Curtain through their own tortures, sufferings, degradation's and final expulsion from Rumania. They were the first to make known to the West the wickedness of communism towards the Gospel believers of all faiths and persuasions. Night after night enthralled, Jonathan listened to the accounts but way far above those was the battle scarred saint himself who had laid his all down for Jesus. That was real, dynamic Christianity: the type that inspired and stirred Jonathan to the depths of his soul. He would get back from the nightly meetings so excited and musing in his spirit how he could help, only to have to face the mundane hum drum of school. How could he do homework after hearing those talks? It was no wonder he worked until 2:00 a.m. every night to get his quota of homework done just so as to be able to attend the meetings again the following night. This was the kind of life Jonathan wanted to live. To be cast upon the God he so desperately loved; believing, trusting, and knowing that He is able in every circumstance. All God needed were men and women who would be big enough to believe Him. "It's for me," he shouted, "for me!"

Each night, supper was forgotten in the urgency to get to the meeting and get a front row pew. He hung on every word. Surely God's Spirit was working inside. This was bigger than just a young man's imagination. This was God Himself moving, testing, proving. The thought of just dropping everything and going really appealed to him but there was school to finish and then university. Short cuts were the answer and with that in mind Jonathan decided how he could knock a year off school and get to University the quicker. There was service to be done for the Lord.

The old steam engine pumped out of Bulawayo station belching smoke and soot into the sultry mid-summer morning. Natives were jostling and shouting - handing huge bundles of belongings through the windows, some live chickens, a bag of corn; running along the platform to throw in the last item to relatives and friends who were leaving on the journey south. The air was pungent with the aroma of hundreds of bodies in the heat and the acrid smell of fermenting fruit. Little kids were rushing along making their last sale to the passengers of boiled corncobs, chickens feet, roasted peanuts and yesterday's buns daubed with icing to make them look fresh. As he waved the final farewell to his family who had become specks in the distance, Jonathan entered his compartment. A new life, new experiences, new friends lay ahead. And, he was running; yes running to do the will of the God he'd come to adore and worship. He was like a volcano ready to erupt with such a burning love and longing to be spent in service for Jesus.

Unbeknown to him, there was a young black boy from Mzilikazi Township. Mzilikazi was named after the Zulu Chief who had fled from King Shaka and made his headquarters at GuBulawayo, the Place of the Elephant" This boy, named Garry, was four years junior to Jonathan and was also running, but he was running from God. His father was a local Pentecostal preacher but that very morning, Garry had stolen money from his Dad's secret nest chuckling to himself because he knew his Dad thought nobody else in the family knew of that hiding place

"Serves him right," Garry had growled, "It's all his fault, I'm sick of church, of his God and prayers. I want to be free and I'm leaving." Without a word, he tied his few clothes into a bundle, grabbed the last of the breakfast bread and left for good. His father was at the church as usual and mother had gone to draw water. They were not poor by everyone else's standards but Garry wanted to be rich and famous. He wanted a bicycle like the white kids he'd seen and to eat ice cream and go to the movies and ride in a car to school. Well, he was going to, no matter what it took....

And there he was, jumping the train to Botswana: angry, frustrated, bitter and vengeful. He was going to join the "Boys" in the bush and come back and fight for everything life had ever denied him. The whispers had been going on for sometime in Mzilikazi that youngsters with weapons were meeting at different places. Then police raids and some arrests had confirmed the whispers. Even his Dad had been questioned about people in his congregation but of course "he knew nothing." Garry thought disparagingly "all he is good for is to tell everyone to love their enemies and to do them good." At that moment Garry felt that the whole world was his enemy - the whites, the blacks, his father, God. He wanted a gun; wanted to be a soldier; a gun would be his friend and give him power. He didn't want to turn back. This was his chance for freedom.

And so, as the old steam train chugged its way to Botswana two young men were on board, each headed for new lives, new destinies, and new horizons. One was running to God and the other away from God. They did not know each other but in time their paths would cross and through a series of incredible events - God ordained events - they would meet and become amazingly, friends.

Jonathan's journey was fifty hours of smoke, dust and soot through the arid dusty Karoo, and finally taking a branch line to the eastern Cape city of Grahamstown, nestled in the mountains. It was raining as the train tried to negotiate the mountain passes. The wheels kept slipping so passengers had to place pebbles of sandstone on the tracks to cause some grip. They walked alongside the train for almost two hours throwing roughage on the line: this was modern South Africa! Finally Grahamstown appeared, the home of the Oxford of the Southern Hemisphere and the ivy walled Rhodes University.

Excitement and thrill tinged with wonder coursed through Jonathan's being as he made his way from the town towards the university. It was set at the top of the town nestled in some hills. What a climb. His legs ached for days as he climbed thousands of steps exploring here and there. Being so young, the university had insisted Jonathan attended "summer school" before registering and so there he was: a whole campus with about two hundred and fifty summer students. It was glorious and the next years were to be some of the happiest in his life. He loved the social life, the academic life and the spiritual life. One key thing happened in each area of life, which would have a major impact on his future, and God would continue to weave the strands that would mold him for later service.

With vigor and gusto Jonathan threw himself into his studies. The volume of work seemed enormous and his choice of subjects were supposed to be for teaching but really befitted administration. He wisely chose each of his first year courses so that they could all be converted into majors and for a laugh, opted for political science. He so loved it that he ended up majoring in it but here was the catch: a vast portion of the course was pure Marxism. Imagine that: studying Marxism in apartheid South Africa in the early 1970's especially its impact on African thinkers and Africa. The university contained all the banned books: Lenin, Marx, Trotsky, Che Guvara, Julius Nyerere, Nkrumah and many modernist Marxists. How well Jonathan remembered having to be specially "REGISTERED" as a political science student for "Special Branch" purposes. Whenever reading the banned books, he would be taken to a prison cell in the basement of the university library, get locked in literally, and then "feed on" the revolutionary Marxists. When finished he would ring a bell and a librarian would come and "set him free."

It was the years of student riots across the world; years when "snotty nosed" liberal kids - the ones who always had the cars, the money, the fast life - wanted to overthrow the status quo but really didn't know why. It was the flower power generation of ban the bomb, love the communists, let's all "love and not war." But Jonathan's country was at real war with communism and Wurmbrand was a living testimony of the evil of a Godless system. While his liberal colleagues marched, were arrested, chased by the police dogs, confronting the law - whether it was national authorities or university authorities - Jonathan became more and more conservative. The more he studied Marxism, the more chaotic and demonic he saw it, embroiling the minds of the multitudes with a false hope and ideals of material utopia on earth. Moscow, Peking, Hanoi, East Berlin belched out the Marxist "dialectic" promising that socialism and then communism would rule the world embracing all mankind in an equal brotherhood. The "exploitation of the masses by the proletariat" would end; "the means of production" would change, "the classless society" would emerge, and "violent revolution" would overthrow each base and superstructure society until the perfect society was established and... and... and here was the key to the whole of Marxism... and "man would know that he is god."

Jonathan's research and reading brought him to the naked truth, "it's the same as the devil offered Adam and Eve in the garden, to become gods...." Then his friend Richard Wurmbrand stumbled across a letter from Marx to His sister. It was found in some archives of the London Library. Marx on his deathbed had revealed his lifelong membership of a satanist society and had written, "I know that I am going to hell. That is where I want to be. But, I am glad that I have left behind a system on earth that will guarantee that the majority of mankind follows me there." Marxism - the full truth; and Jonathan spent three years studying its workings, its advocates and he would experience its realities. It was not different in any way to the Nazism of Adolph Hitler.

Meantime across hundreds of miles little Garry found his camp. He was starved, beaten, insulted and ridiculed, all in the name of the cause. Awakened at 3:00 a.m. daily for physicals, he was forced on the most excruciating runs and physical fitness programs. If he didn't perform he was beaten and tortured and made to repeat. It was agony, punishment, cruelty of the worst kind. It was not what he had expected. At first he cried - quietly at night for fear of being found out - but soon he became hardened. So why did he endure? Why did he willingly submit to the nightmare ordeals that would haunt him for years? Because they would kill him if he ran away and because of his real friend: they slept together at night; suffered together by day; ate together and played together. His friend had real power. Garry proved himself through all the ordeals and had waited patiently for the promise; the promise of that friend who wouldn't leave him, forsake him, ditch him, let him down. The friend who would change life and give him all he'd ever wanted was the real friend with power and had a name: AK 47.

It was one year later after joining up - when Jonathan was entering his second year of political studies and would really get his teeth into Marx - that Garry, who had really proven himself and shown himself to be above his colleagues for sheer guts, determination, anger, hatred and aggression was chosen for Prague, Belgrade, East Berlin and Moscow. He'd made it and was about to embark on his courses in Marxist indoctrination: how to kill, create carnage, torture, instill fear, lay landmines and destroy and overthrow the "means of production." Violent revolution, violent rhetoric, violent living. Gratify the senses and live for today: take all you want by violent force and nobody will stop you because real power is "with the barrel of a gun...." Little did he realize that, like multitudes of others, he was a mere pawn in the hands of unscrupulous men, who themselves, were pawns in the hands of an unscrupulous devil. But, Garry would love the veneer: the uniforms, the "comrade" this and "comrade" that; the weapons and the hatred for those who had "exploited" him; little realizing that his new masters who appeared as "brothers" were the real ruthless exploiters.

Back in Grahamstown in his walk with the Lord, Jonathan entertained the nagging feeling that something was missing. There was a greater dimension of Jesus. What was it? He threw himself into every area of Christian activity both on campus and in the local Baptist Church. He avoided the heated religious debates among the theological students. Calvinism, fundamentalism, Armenianism all sounded too much like communism and were not for him. He joined the Rag Committee and became president elect of the S.R.C. on the grounds of ousting N.U.S.A.S. - the National Union of Students, a political organ of the communist A.N.C. - African National Congress. These moves plunged Jonathan into a major crisis with his Church which vehemently disapproved and isolated him. Piloting him through these series of seemingly catastrophic events, the Holy Spirit visited him and Jonathan became a "tongue talker." And so, a whole new dynamic wave broke upon his life and jettisoned Jonathan into new excitement, increased faith and a deeper walk with the Lord Jesus. He was in the clouds for months, walking on air, in love, excited. It was almost as if a veil had been torn away and God had become so real, so close and so intimate. There was no religion; it was relationship. Pentecost was a DYNAMIC that exploded in Jonathan's life. He had an even greater desire to "do something" for the Lord but all in good time. University was fun, stimulating and opening up new worlds and avenues.

Finals were fast approaching and new opportunities awaited Jonathan for postgraduate studies. He had excelled in History and had been invited to read Honors. He was president of the new S.R.C. for the next year; chairman of the Rag Committee, a university celebrity and known and respected by faculty and students alike. He mapped out his program with care BUT the Lord disapproved. The first morning of finals, as he knelt to pray, that same light Jonathan had experienced at conversion streamed into his room. God began to speak. "Jonathan, you said you were going to serve Me. Have you changed your mind? Choose Me or university."

"No Lord! It's You."

"Then this is the end of the road here. Today I will give you your degree and you will never get another academic qualification. I will teach you...."

With that, He was gone and as only God can engineer things He prevented Jonathan's return to university the following year. Ended was the Rag Chairmanship, S.R.C. Presidency, the Honors degree.

The "Fasten Seat Belt" sign twinkled on as the hostess announced, "We are about to land at London's Heathrow...." Jonathan didn't hear the rest. The jet had been flying in over London with its teeming millions. "How many know the Lord?" thought Jonathan. "What multitudes of lost and dying, going nowhere?"

His worst fears seemed realized as he saw churches turned into Bingo halls; signs "Save the Church Tombola." This was the England which had sent out the great missionaries, stood against Rome, won the nations for Jesus. This was the England of winning the lost; it weighed him down and he was not even there for that purpose. He carried one letter of introduction: "Richard Wurmbrand Christian Mission to the Communist World." He'd come to train and work as a Bible smuggler in the days before it became "fashionable". Days when the communists were making strides in Africa, in Asia, in South America and Europe and Britain; when the cold war had not yet begun to wax against them and they were arrogant and aggressive. Those were the days when a Bible smuggler if caught, would join the ranks of Solzhenietsen's "Gulag" and little if anything was done. Jonathan's Mother's bitter tears and her fear that "you will end up in Siberia and we'll never see you again..." could not dissuade him. And so, he had embarked, signed on, was prepared for it all no matter what "it" was.

Months of ministering, learning, working, preparing, followed but everything suddenly ended when Jonathan had a significant encounter. Finding himself back in London for a brief respite he had continued to be weighed down by the lost ness of the people. Everyone he spoke to seemed disinterested in the God he so loved. London was especially hard. The vastness of reaching a lost, cold and casual world weighed upon him. For days he walked the streets trying to talk, minister and convince people of a loving Savior, but to no avail.

One morning early, his heart crushing for the lost, Jonathan made his way down towards Thames Bridge. The only people about were the milkmen. It was cool and there was a mist swirling along the Embankment. Somewhere, and he doesn't remember the exact spot, there was a small triangular area of well - trimmed lawn bordered by flowers. A park bench was situated on the close edge and there, eating an apple, sat one who appeared to be an old man. Jonathan was in great travail of soul but made his way toward this seeming "beggar" for he looked roughly dressed. Nobody else was in sight. "Excuse me Sir," said Jonathan, "Do you know my Jesus?"

"I vividly recall the sequence of events," said he in later years. The man reached out and took my hand saying, `My child, I AM the Son of God.' His reply did not immediately strike me but what did was that my whole being turned liquid as it were and there was a burning inside of me just as the two disciples had experienced on the road to Emmaus. Excitement, joy, peace, poured through my body and I wanted to leap, shout and dance all at the same time. I felt as if I could cartwheel and flick flack all over London. Without any other words I drew away from the man, turned my back on him to continue my walk. I was too elated to be rational. Suddenly I stopped. I was compelled to give that man everything I had and took my entire worldly wealth amounting to ten pounds from my pocket. I turned to give it to him and he was gone; I could see in every direction despite the mist and he had not walked off: he'd clearly disappeared.

Still, the impact of what had happened did not dawn on me; not even his disappearance. Might well He have said to me "ye slow of heart to believe," but I was floating in air as if drunken like the Apostles on the day of Pentecost. I laughed, cried and ran all at the same time. I wanted to go to heaven right away. The world seemed like an unreal place and I felt as though I did not belong here.

I found myself on Thames Bridge looking down into the slick, slow - flowing river and then for the first time began to ponder in my heart. Suddenly an audible voice called my name, "Jonathan, Jonathan," so that I spun around to see who had crept up on me unawares. I knew nobody in London. There was nobody, but the voice continued: "Jonathan, I want you to return to your Homeland and serve Me. I will send you to the east of your land and there you will die for Me." It was enough. Suddenly I knew that I had met the Lord Himself. He hadn't disappeared but had followed me down on to Thames Bridge and given me my battle orders. What an awesome meeting."

"Well Jonathan, congratulations. With your degree we'll commission you immediately with the rank of Cadet District Officer. Now let me see, there are seventy-six vacancies throughout the country. What is your preference for a posting?"

"Matabeleland, Sir, where I grew up." (That is in the west of Rhodesia). "Alright. Go back to Bulawayo and report to the District Commissioner in four days and he'll have your posting. Good luck!"

Jonathan had joined Internal Affairs. This was the administrative wing of the Government, responsible for overseeing operations in the vast rural districts of Rhodesia. It was the type of life he loved. Being in the bush was appealing but what was to follow was quite unexpected.

"You are posted to Umtali and the Eastern border districts," said the District Commissioner (D.C.). Jonathan never heard another word. The only thing that echoed through his mind as the D.C. rambled on was: "I will send you to the East... you will die for Me there." "It's really you, Lord," mused Jonathan.... So collect your warrant and catch the train. Report on Monday to the D.C. Umtali." It was final. Indeed, when God ordains something it cannot be changed. He had spoken and His Word was final. How awesome is our God who ordains the affairs of men. The nations are a drop in the bucket to Him BUT the very hairs of our head are numbered, and in the vast affairs of the infinite cosmos, God can still be concerned with the destiny of one person, one young man whose heart is inclined towards Him.

"Sa! Sa! The count. Ten dead and four injured. We've tied up the injured and put them under guard," reported Sgt. Khami. Jonathan wasn't listening but Khami's voice snapped him back to the reality of the situation. So here he was, commander of this whole outfit and administrator on the field of two of the most terr - infested districts in Rhodesia: Maranke and Zimunya Tribal Trust Lands, both on the eastern border with Mocambique.

The sound of choppers beating the air announced the arrival of the trackers. They would also take out the men and prisoners. "Perhaps the army will respect us now, Sgt., that was quite a kill rate for this unit." "Them! `Suta Nyorka,'" his Ndebele tongue clicked. He used one of the worst swear expressions in the language, "their mother's are snakes."

"Sgt. Khami!" Jonathan rebuked, "that's not the language of a prince from the royal house of Lobengula."

CHAPTER THREE

DEATH'S JAWS

The Leopard sped down the sandy road of what had become Jonathan's personal racetrack. No, the Leopard was not a wild animal of the cat family but an ingeniously designed mine protected vehicle which looked like a "V" on wheels. The "V" was made of armor plated tracer - proof steel and could seat six men on two bench seats plus a driver whose vision was through a small slit window of three inch armor - plated glass.

The road was a gentle decline which led down to a river some eight miles away. The vehicle was normally very slow but with the weight and the downhill Jonathan was rapidly gaining momentum. The African dusk was settling in and he must reach base by night.

Without warning as he sped along he saw, as if someone was showing him a movie through the lens of a zoom camera, the road up four miles ahead. The "film" picked out all the characteristic landmarks; rocks, trees, bushes that he knew so well. He saw each bend in the road as the film took him down and across the dry river bed. Then, ascending the opposite bank the lens zoomed in on a big tree. Jonathan had always marveled at the hugeness of the tree and its vast canopy spreading large pools of cool shade in the African sun. In peaceful times it would be lovely to picnic there. Then the film zeroed in on the road. Jonathan looked and suddenly realized. There was a landmine right under the tree. The camera showed him the exact location. On up the hill the film progressed, picking out a small native trading store. Again the camera zoomed in on the shop. The doors were closed and bolted; the windows shuttered. Through the doors the camera went. Inside in the darkness of the room there was a small tin with a paraffin wick burning and emitting a faint smoldering light. The wick needed trimming. Jonathan marveled at the detail. Men lay around on straw mats. He saw AK 47 rifles, RPD rockets and their launchers, grenades, RPG machine guns, magazines and ammo belts. The men were eating and drinking. Outside at the back of the store the camera zoomed in on the storeowner and his wife who were cooking over an open fire. That too was unusual. A man did not cook when his wife was present - he must have been forced to do so by the terrs who had obviously intimidated the couple into entertaining them.

Just as it had started, the movie suddenly stopped and so did Jonathan. The leopard slid to a halt. He threw her into neutral and yanked on the handbrake. "What do we do Lord?" he asked. "Proceed. You'll be all right but don't engage," came the gentle but reassuring whisper.

"Sa! Sa! What is it?" shouted Sgt. Khami excitedly.

"Ambush? Landmine? Gandanga?" gibbered Corporal Kizito (Gandanga was the colloquial Shona term for terrorists). "Relax, relax," said Jonathan holding up his hands as he began to explain what he had seen. It was incredible.

Sgt. Khami was a huge 6' 5" muscular native. He was very black and his broad shoulders and enormous arms and thighs allowed him to pick up three hundred pounds with ease. He was descended from the royal Zulu line of Shaka from whom his great grandfather had fled with Mzilikazi to establish the Royal Ndebele House. In size he was worth two of the Corporal who was a traditional Shona. Though Sgt. and Corporal had learned to get along with each other under the continual watchful eye of Jonathan, Khami made no secret that he despised the Shona. They had always been the traditional vassals of the war-like Matabele. Khami was a noble man and a noble fighter. He loved and respected heroism and enjoyed danger. He'd become like a shadow to Jonathan whose side he never left even to go on "R" and "R" (Rest and Recreation). His royal dignity and Ndebele blood would not permit him to eat with the other men or even drink from the same water bottle as they but he would on occasions eat with Jonathan. There was a bonding between this noble prince and his white commander, stimulated because the latter always referred to himself not as a Rhodesian but a Matabele. This made Khami greatly proud deep down.

As Jonathan recounted what he'd seen, Khami was already grabbing his rifle. He loved a fight especially if it meant inflicting damage on "these cowardly Shona terrs." His frame was already shaking with excitement and anticipation.

"No! No!" spoke Jonathan emphatically. "The Lord says no fighting."

"But Nkulu Nkhosi," began Khami.... He always used the Ndebele salute of "Royal Chief" when he wanted to greatly pressure Jonathan for his own way.

"No Sergeant. It's final. The Lord says NO." His men had learned to respect and fear the Lord through their commander. They held in awe that he heard from God in matters like this. Too often he had warned them of ambushes up ahead, of landmines or attacks. He'd always been right and always made sure they knew it was God who had told him.

The men had watched Jonathan's life carefully. Their commander never swore or cursed like others. They never saw him touch a beer or smoke a cigarette. He often left his fellow whites when they began their "nonsense talk" and would make his way quietly to his men whom he would engage in conversation usually about Jesus. They knew he loved Jesus and was always excited about Him. They'd seen him quietly praying and his batman had reported to them that he had overheard the "Boss" speaking their names to God when he did not know he was being overheard. Jonathan was tough and could really shout when necessary - I guess he inherited his father's parade-ground voice - but his men didn't mind that because they knew he really loved them. The proof of it was evident. He always visited their families and ate with them when in town, provided medicine when they were sick and was always known to help when his men were financially in trouble as long as it wasn't because of drinking. He taught them to be responsible and to learn to be mature. They'd seen him quietly cry over the loss of any one of his men in battle and fearlessly defend them before the army leaders. Internal Affairs and the army never got along but they had seen more action than most of the army. Their job was not supposed to be military but civilian administration though they had been thrown into a military role and a self-taught one at that! In the beginning they had done their job effectively without mine protected vehicles. It had been several months before Jonathan and his men had even received automatic weapons. How faithful had been the Lord to watch over and protect the group. They had already become a legend and unknown to them, they were being hunted because of Jonathan and his God. The terrs had pitted their demon gods against the power of Christ. It was a spiritual war in very natural circumstances.

With that, Jonathan engaged gear and off they sped, following the road down to the river. They were acutely alert. The eyes of his four men were like wide saucers, their whites showing against dark black faces. Crossing the dry riverbed which became a raging torrent in the rains, Jonathan swung the vehicle far across to the right as they passed under the tree. Even as he did, he winced and tensed as if waiting for the explosion which never came. He'd seen the damage of many a landmine. He'd witnessed them in action. They were hated. They were destructive. They were cowardly things. They did not differentiate between civilian and military vehicles but then the terrs didn't care. Theirs was a reign of terror. They massacred, raped and tortured the people into submission.

The Leopard passed the store, climbed to the brow of the hill and sped off into the fast darkening night. "Phew!" Everyone breathed a sigh of relief.

Back at camp, Jonathan found Rusty van Skalkwyk. "Rusty" was appropriate for he looked like a rusty burned nail. If it had been the days of AIDS one would have thought he was dying from it. He was a mixture of all races, a chain smoker and "pickled" from years of hard drinking. He hated Jonathan, hated his religion, hated his popularity, just plain hated him. Behind his back he referred to Jonathan with contempt as "Kaffir Boetie." It was a derogatory Afrikaans term for those who befriended the blacks. Jonathan never understood why he worked for A. D. F. (African Development Fund, the branch of Internal Affairs which dealt with development in the Tribal Trust Lands, building schools, clinic, roads, bridges) since he hated the black people so much. Rusty was already "under the weather" (drunk) from his fourth or fifth brandy and was ultra obnoxious. He was showing off in front of another equally drunk "old timer" who looked as if he'd been kicked in the chest and was a walking "question mark". They were already slurring together as they waited for supper.

Jonathan usually ate alone except when top brass came. His own "chef" whom he had carefully trained prepared his food. He was particular, insisting on white tablecloth and fine bone china even in the most remote areas. Since Jonathan was effectively in charge, he made sure that everything was done in order. Rusty hated that too. Unfortunately, Internal Affairs officials except the District Commissioner could not command A.D.F. personnel.

"Evening Rusty."

"Ugh" he grunted.

"Are you leaving early in the morning?" Jonathan asked politely.

"You in a hurry to get rid of me out of you... camp?" Rusty muttered.

"No Rusty but I have to warn you about a landmine which the terrs have planted under that great 'ntonga tree by the river."

"How d'ya know, boy?" Rusty drawled.

Jonathan knew when Rusty called him "boy" that he was in a particularly off-hand mood. Swallowing hard for he sensed what was coming, Jonathan continued; "Rusty, for once you have got to believe me. I know it's there, I saw it."

"Did you stop and look?"

"Well no, Rusty."

"Then how d'ya see it?"

"The Lord showed me Rusty and I have to warn you..."

"Don't give me any of your... Baby Jesus religious junk...."

"That's enough of that Rusty," shouted Jonathan, "I'm telling you, warning you: don't take that new truck on that road tomorrow until I get the engineers to clear it. I know there is a landmine there and I'm going to radio now."

"You won't get through 'til morning," Rusty growled.

"I'll try any call sign. Good night."

At first light next day Jonathan was up early to take Corporal Kizito and Lazarus out to do some ground security work. They would move through the villages picking up information on the whereabouts of terrs. Lazarus had been nick-named "Come forth" by Jonathan after Jesus' miracle in calling Lazarus forth from the tomb and because Jonathan had had a prophetic word that Lazarus would, in fact, come forth out of the jaws of death.

It was another cold winter morning just a week after the ambush. Several of the men were squatting around fires warming their hands when Jonathan came outside. The sergeant saluted as he opened the door of the Leopard.

"Khami, tell Mr. Rusty's driver to come here. He mustn't leave before the road is cleared even if Mr. Rusty wants to go."

"Sa, we tell him already. He say he no go fa sha."

"Okay then, let us be going."

The Leopard took off in the opposite direction to where the landmine had been sighted and Jonathan was gone two hours, timing himself to get back just in time to make first radio communication with Umtali. The truck was gone.

"The fool," shouted Jonathan, "the idiot!"

His men were all standing around, shaking their heads, tutting and talking excitedly.

"Is the radio on?"

"Yes Sa."

"I told the driver not to go..."

"Sa driver is here..." said Sgt. Khami.

"Call him," Jonathan ordered.

Jumu, the driver came running but kept his distance. He acted very sheepishly "Masta, masta, I refuse but he, Mr. Rusty, he slap me an' taken the keys..."

"O Lord," was all Jonathan could groan.

"May Day. May Day," the radio crackled.

"There it is - get ready quickly Sgt.," ordered Jonathan as he ran for the radio.

"May Day - Shumba Loc 2 receiving you strength 3 over."

"May Day hit Lima Mike. Request casavac, repeat request casavac urgently, over."

"Copied May Day. Be on guard for Tangos. Help on its way over."

"May Day over and out."

Jonathan switched the dials of the powerful S.S.B. radio and spoke with authority.

"Pappa Alpha Delta One, this is Shumba May Day do you read, over."

"Shumba fives, over."

"Yes Pappa Alpha Delta One. Rusty collected Lima Mike loc figures 642930 map Echo Charlie figures 21 Charlie Delta site river by store. Request emergency casavac chopper and back up troops. Possible Tangos. Send trackers. Send wrecker."

"Shumba copied. Transmitting immediately by landline, over."

"Pappa Alpha Delta One, Shumba on immediate follow-up. Stay on frequency, out."

"Roger Shumba, out."

"Khami, take the Crocodile with twenty men. Corporal Benson, remain here and guard the base. Put all men on Alert Red until I return. You could get attacked while we're gone. Keep radio comms."

Jonathan prayed over his men and they moved out. The terrs would anticipate a follow up and could be waiting in ambush, have laid another mine or be thirty miles away or even outside the base waiting. Jonathan's blood boiled. This is what he really hated. The enemy seldom ever faced in clean battle, it was always hit and run! As they arrived at the scene the choppers began circling and firing off bursts from the mounted machine guns.

"Sgt. take up defensive positions. Also, arrest the store keeper and his wife and hand them to special branch at base."

"Yes Sa," Khami grinned. He was always thrilled at times like that. Jonathan prayed he would surrender to the Lord but something was holding him back. The vehicle was a mess. One entire wheel was lodged in the tree. The cab was pulverized. If it hadn't been for the armor plating underneath, Rusty and his friend Brent would not have survived. As it was, Rusty lay unconscious with his legs badly broken and lacerated. Brent had some long gashes on his thigh and blood and glass on his face. He was in major shock. The casavac chopper landed and the medics rushed out while the second chopper circled, concentrating on a small rocky hill just off the road. There seemed no likelihood of an ambush then. Besides, the terrs were terrified of helicopters and usually fled at the first sound of them. In minutes the injured were on drips, strapped down and loaded into the chopper.

Jonathan knew that it was useless to try and speak above the noise of the rotors and engine and he also knew that the second chopper would land and let off trackers as soon as the casavac was away. The helicopter rose, poised for a second, turned 180 degrees and moved off. To his horror and dismay the second chopper followed. Where were the trackers? Grabbing the radio he shouted into it, "Pappa Alpha Delta One, Shumba, do you read?"

"Shumba fives, go," came Rita's voice clearly. Women's voices with their higher pitch were always much clearer than men's on the radio.

"Pappa Alpha Delta One requested trackers. What's going on? There are Tangos at this loc, over."

"Shumba: Delta Charlie at Juliet Oscar Charlie now."

"That's not good enough," shouted Jonathan, "What about wrecker?"

"En route your loc. What of Rusty?"

"Not good but on his way. Hino a mess. Will remain at this loc for wrecker. Make comms as soon as Delta Charlie arrives your loc."

"Roger."

"Shumba out."

"Pappa Alpha Delta One out."

The whole road, the remains of the Hino truck and the bushes were covered with black from the explosion. The steel plating under the cab was twisted and the explosion had forced the cab up at almost a right angle to the bed of the truck. Diesel had leaked all over the road. It was one big mess and Jonathan wondered whether Rusty's attitude would change after this experience.

"You really gave him a chance Lord," he whispered. "What a God you are!" The Sergeant was by his side. A little away stood two district assistants guarding the shop owner and his wife who were handcuffed together. "Put them in the Crocodile Khami and radio base to see if everything's okay."

"Sa," said Khami as he gave the order and went to the radio. Jonathan sat in the shade of the big tree as the radio crackled and Khami began transmitting. Jonathan did not hear the rest. He became lost in awe and wonder at the God he loved and His mighty saving power. "That landmine was for us... You saved us Lord. Thank you, thank you. I adore You."

It had been a long hard day by the time Jonathan returned to base after dark. The wrecker had arrived unescorted. Jonathan had been furious. The brass in town thought this was some kind of game going on. He would have to make a trip to Umtali to lay the cards on the table. "Next week", he decided. They had had to escort the wrecker fifty miles to the paved road and come back to base about another eighty miles. Jonathan was tired and went to bed immediately after his bath and dinner. It was cold and he snuggled under his four warm blankets, rifle right next to him. He had decided on maintaining Red Alert. Something made him uneasy. He was just about to fall asleep when the familiar voice of the Lord commanded: "Jonathan get up and check the fence."

"Not tonight Lord - it's okay. Besides, everybody is on Red Alert. We'll be fine."

"No, check it," He insisted.

"Well Lord, I'm really tired and everyone's on duty."

"I said check it. Do it NOW," He demanded.

Instantly Jonathan was wide-awake. He had learned to obey that voice - it was the difference between life and death. He went to the control room and to his horror found the fence alarm switch in the "off" position. A huge fence with an electric pulse surrounded the camp so that if anyone touched or cut it a siren would immediately begin to wail. The sound of the siren alone was enough to frighten anyone.

He switched on. The siren began to wail. He pressed the various buttons but the siren still continued. Outside everybody had grabbed his rifle and was instantly alert. The Sgt. came running, barking orders left and right. "It's okay Khami, there must be a short, but why wasn't it reported? Where's the fence boy? Punish him for this. He knows the rules. Bring a detail and let's check the fence."

By torchlight it was both very difficult and dangerous, as they became sitting targets for anyone who was outside the fence. But, there was nothing else to do. As they progressed around the fence, Jonathan was himself getting alarmed. Something had to be the matter. "Show me Lord," he silently prayed, "You woke me up."

Arriving finally at the last corner post having circuited the whole fence, Jonathan's torch picked up the thinnest copper wire linking the alarm wire to the diamond mesh fence. It was so insignificant that they could easily have missed it and it was placed in such a way so as to look like an accident. It was however, deliberate. Jonathan sensed the danger as he removed the wire and he was subconsciously aware that he was being watched from outside the fence. It was no wonder the boy had missed such a fine wire even in broad daylight, but he should have reported it. Jonathan was exhausted and his feelings didn't clearly translate to his rational mind.

Having settled the matter and switched on the fence to find it working perfectly, Jonathan retired again after giving last warning orders to Khami. He fell into a deep slumber, an unusually deep sleep.

The first mortar exploded right outside Jonathan's lounge window sending glass flying and stones rattling down the roof. Jonathan leapt horizontally out of bed and hit the floor. He was in such a deep sleep that for a split second he wondered where he was. Usually he never slept like that. The sound of a breaking twig would normally have him instantly alert. He had become disciplined to light sleeping. "It would have to be tonight," he groaned, "that I slept like that."

Mortars were already exploding everywhere and the rattle of machine guns and rifle fire was deafening.

Slipping on shoes and spectacles in one move, Jonathan grabbed his rifle and rushed from the room on to the verandah (porch) of his little cottage. Tracer bullets were flying in all directions, mortar bombs exploding, rockets whizzing through the air and bursting into flame on impact. There seemed a hundred AK 47's flashing from outside the fence. His men were replying, the siren was wailing. The cold night was thrown into chaos.

Jonathan was instantly thrown on to the floor and pinned down. He couldn't even lift his head. He wrestled and struggled but couldn't move. Bullets were bombarding away his verandah walls, exploding on the cement pillars, sending chips flying and smashing windows. A rocket whistled through the verandah, its rear fin catching a pillar and tearing a gash in it. The thing exploded on a tree. Mortars were still exploding and sending up debris and flashes. Fortunately, whoever had paced off the target that day had made a major mistake. All the mortars were falling wide of their targets.

Suddenly Jonathan knew, knew beyond all doubt that an angel was holding him down. He couldn't see because he was held face-down on the ground but he could feel the hand on his head. The angel he felt had sat on him and he was fixed, immovable. Minutes seemed like hours and all he wanted was to fight back, take command, hit the enemy. The AK 47 fire suddenly stopped. Jonathan's men were still firing. At that moment Jonathan was released and turned in time to see the glowing figure of a huge angel disappearing. The angel looked back over his shoulder and sweetly smiled in a knowing fashion. It was no hallucination, no mistake, no trick of the eye in battle. Then he remembered his mother recounting how granddad had been at the Battle on Mons during World War I. The British had lost thousands of men. Only a handful remained against enormous German odds. The men, not particularly Godly, had prayed that night asking God for help. At dawn the next day, the sky was full of angels. The British won (in battle that followed) against those incredible German odds.

Freed then Jonathan advanced towards the fence, dodging like a rabbit from tree to building to tree. Finally he crawled on his belly to within six feet of the fence firing as he went. He could hear the terrs then. They were packing up and moving off. They usually didn't stay too long especially if they were met with a reply of strong fire power. "Typically cowardly - hit and run," sighed Jonathan. Sgt. Khami crept up whispering "Nkosi, Nkosi," until he was beside Jonathan. "I think its over, Khami."

"Too much today, Sir. Those gandanga are ...."

The siren was still wailing and had become so infuriating that Jonathan himself felt like putting a bullet through it. The odd shot from his men still rang out. It was time again when the eyes played tricks and the trees began to move. It was cold and for the first time Jonathan started shivering. It was a mixture of the weather, the angel and the attack.

"Khami, go switch off that siren. Detail the corporals to account for their men. I pray there are no dead. They were firing rather high except at my cottage." Soon the siren stopped and the stillness of the African night returned. Some considerable distance off Jonathan heard the terrs singing one of their revolutionary songs. They were rejoicing and confident that Jonathan was dead. He could not possibly have survived such an attack. They knew nobody would give chase and he knew they were all gone. None would dare to stay around - they had to reach their hiding places before daylight when they expected choppers and trackers and the crack Selous Scouts of whom they were terrified to start hunting them. Little did the terrs or Jonathan know at that stage that they wouldn't be coming. Jonathan gave the "all clear" and walked back to his corporals who were gathering to report. One District Assistant had a bad flesh wound and several had minor cuts and scratches. With that information Jonathan gave the orders: "Medic, put the D.A. on drips, clean and dress the wound, shoot him with morphine and antibiotics and make sure that the bullet is out. Sgt., set the details. We stay on Red."

"Sa." Jonathan could hear the Sgt. barking the orders as he made his way back to his cottage. Fortunately his bedroom on the south side (the attack was from the north) was intact. His batman was trying to clean up the lounge. "Charles, go tell the Sgt. I've gone to bed and to call me if he needs me. Then you clean up this mess in the morning." "Yes, Sir," he replied grinning. "We very lucky tonight. Very sure those gandangas want to kill you Sir but I know Jesus taken care of you."

Jonathan crawled back into the warmth of the blankets. It was 0230 and the whole ordeal had lasted about an hour. "Thank you, thank you, Lord." he said as he dozed off. But he couldn't sleep. He kept having visions of the huge angel. "Why, Lord?" he asked, "I thought you said I was going to die out here."

The simple reply of God came softly, "I love you. You will know."

"O Father, I love you too. I adore you. I'm crazy about you Lord." Jonathan was so excited as he thought of the angel he started bouncing in bed but decided against shouting out lest everyone should think, "Attack!" His mind was cast back to London. It wasn't that he was looking for these things to happen. He was excitedly, delightedly in love with Jesus. They were just happening. Jonathan did not debate the theology, he accepted simply and without questioning. He had such peace in the midst of all this. It was a marvel that God who said he would "die" was doing the utmost to keep him alive. It was beyond reasoning, so he didn't even try.

First light found Jonathan surveying the damage and he could see the reason for the angelic encounter. His verandah was in the direct line of a large portion of the firepower. The wall was almost totally blasted away. They obviously knew his cottage. There must be an informer. If he had lifted his head so much as a couple of inches, he would have had it taken clear off. He simply marveled at how the Lord had saved him from the jaws of death yet again. The Lord knew that he didn't fear and didn't really care. He had taken extraordinary measures to protect one ordinary person who believed in the mightiness of an awesome God.

The morning was spent radioing and clearing up. There was actually surprisingly little damage. No choppers were coming so one of the corporals was detailed to drive the injured D.A. to hospital - a round trip of two hundred and fifty miles. "Watch for landmines. Drive center and side," Jonathan cautioned. "Report to the District Commissioner when you get to town and radio me."

"Sa."

Jonathan poured over his maps, calculating, analyzing and detailing logistics of where terrs might be and their estimated numbers. Was there one big detachment or many smaller ones? Were the terrs who laid the landmine the same as those who attacked last night? Who was feeding them? Where was their supply route? This was all vital information Jonathan wanted at his fingertips. He wanted to go on the offensive again. Was it all the work of the famous Kufa Ufulu?

It was almost 1130 hours when Khami rushed in breathless, "Sir, you better come quickly. It's Lazarus. He's back but no Kizito."

Lazarus was sitting under a tree soaked in sweat and ashen gray. His shirt and trousers were ripped and his arms torn and bleeding. He tried to rise but was completely spent. He was still gasping for breath, his chest heaving. He tried to talk but it was impossible. Great rasping breaths could not ease the heaving of his chest as he groaned in pain.

"Get water. Soak him down. When he can talk, call me. Get the medic and fix those wounds."

Jonathan went back to his maps and it was sometime before Lazarus appeared at his office.

"Sir," he saluted. He looked a little more composed and was breathing normally. He'd washed and changed. He sat and excitedly began to tell his incredible escape, filling in the details as he went. Jonathan already had the map in front him, marking points and making notes as Lazarus talked. At times Lazarus choked back the tears and Jonathan turned his own head as tears ran down his cheeks. The account was moving.

"We arrived near McBride Bridge last night after moving through Sabukus Divani; Mbame, Manaketsi and Petropini. He's a snake and feeds gandangas. There's plenty evidence of a strong presence; maybe one hundred or more. Well, this morning we went to Mai Chitonga's trading store. She has too many goods, Sir. She talks a lot and when we wanted to go she gives us food and cokes. I suddenly realized she's keeping us there so I grab Kizito and we run out. It was too late. Gandangas were already close, maybe fifty yards. We run and they start shooting. They chase us very fast, Kizito was behind but I saw him trip and fall. They were too close to him. I ran on and didn't stop until reaching here. I saw them catch Kizito...and...and..." he wept.

"Man, that's thirty miles. We'll have to enter you for the marathon."

"Sir, if they get Kizito, they make him talk, he stammered." "I know Lazarus, but maybe we can do something." Jonathan was very choked up because he had really grown to love Kizito. "Sgt. let's go. Put Benson on Red Alert again and bring thirty D. A.'s in the Crocodile." The Crocodile was a Toyota ten-ton truck built up around the sides with steel plating and firing slots. The cab had no doors. It was completely armor plated and the driver slid into his seat from the top. It looked a menacing vehicle. "Watch for landmines and make sure you follow in my tracks. Bring two cases of ammo, radios, medicals."

"Sa" saluted Khami who was in his element and with obvious enjoyment. This kind of action made life for Khami worth living. "This will be our strategy," Jonathan explained, showing them on the map.... "Detail all the men and groups to take up immediate positions on arrival...."

"Sa." He left snapping orders at the corporals who in turn barked at the men. Lazarus was in the Leopard with Jonathan. "Well you certainly are `Come forth' eh," said Jonathan. "Obviously the Lord has something for you. You'd better surrender to Him now. Right out of the jaws of death ha?"
"Yes Sir, I think so," was all he could say smiling broadly. He felt like a man with a new release, a second chance. It was an hour's drive. They went slow in case of mines but Jonathan really knew in his heart that some local traders like Mai Chitonga and Petropini and others were paying the terrs not to mine the roads so they could continue with their lucrative businesses. The buses no longer traveled these areas so people could not get to town easily and were forced to rely on such unscrupulous traders who fleeced them to feed the terrs. Mai Chitonga would be arrested, her store closed and goods confiscated.
On their arrival "nobody" had observed gandangas, heard firing or seen running men. The local headman denied everything emphatically yet he was only seventy yards from the store. Seeing the man's little boy of about four years Jonathan squatted and cajoled him over with candy. He played with him for a few minutes until the child was relaxed. Then swinging him on to one knee he bounced him up and down. He allowed him to hold his rifle. The kid was then very proud as his snotty nosed brothers and sisters and friends gathered around. When Jonathan took off his hat and put it on the boy's head, the child thought he was really important. "Lazarus, now ask him gently if he saw anything this morning." At first he haltingly said he'd seen soldiers. There was shooting. More soldiers. Men running. Soon all the kids joined in the story trying to be important and outdo their friends with detail. There were about twenty children and more were coming. Some of the older children became explicit in their details of how the terrs had raped the women, eaten their food and drunk at the store. When finally satisfied with the accounts, Jonathan said to a D.A.: "Take them all to the store and give each one a handful of candy by courtesy of Mai Chitonga."
Jonathan called Khami, "Detail some men to round up these people and Mai Chitonga and put them under guard. Give out liberally from her shop - the rest, place in the Crocodile." This was war! "If anyone runs shoot, but mind the kids. Tell them to take their candy, give them some biscuits (cookies) too and go and play far

away. There could be shooting. Then Khami, bring a detail and come with me. We're going to track...."

This was the worst part of the bloody terr war; the involvement of innocent children. Typically those youngsters had seen the worst of humanity as the terrs had pillaged their villages and raped mothers, daughters, sisters. Their wickedness knew no restraints. They ate food meant for the children, shot any who were reluctant to co-operate and tortured their fathers at will. Often the children had been forced to watch in horror. Occasionally when a youngster became hysterical at what was being perpetrated on his parents the terrs would not hesitate to bayonet such a child and silence him forever. What wickedness; what savagery what a senseless carnage. One day, those sadists and destroyers of humanity would become world heroes. In the meantime they continued their reign of terror and it was the innocent children who suffered more than anyone. The horrendous scenes of the war indelibly scarred their delicate minds. They would awake at night screaming in fear as the images of terrible experiences came back to haunt them over and over. There was no respite. Jonathan realized that they were all - including himself - victims of a senseless war, the real masters of which sat in their luxurious palaces in overseas capitals.

Khami was almost like a schoolboy with delight. The kids had pointed the direction in which the terrs had gone and Jonathan and his detail began to follow. There was abundant evidence of terr activity and Jonathan was fast drawing the conclusion that this was a large group and would require the army. There were strong indications that they had the full support of the whole area. Cattle had been deliberately driven along their route to cover tracks. The search was taking them to some very rocky hills. They came to a "V" shaped valley bounded by hills of enormous balancing rocks on both sides and thickly forested with thorn shrubs. At the end of the valley was an open field with some huts looking suspiciously deserted. Jonathan was convinced that the terrs were there or had recently visited the huts. The hair rose on Jonathan's neck. "This is it," he said to Khami as he ordered a halt. "I can smell them, I can feel them." Jonathan sent four men ahead to scout with instructions that if they got through the valley they should take up defensive positions on the other side. Jonathan felt his hands sticky on his rifle as he began to sweat. Sgt. Khami was shuffling agitatedly, longing for action. It was electrifying. The men moved cautiously, slowly. Any second Jonathan expected the whine of an RPD rocket or the rattle of an RPG7 machine gun. The four scouts, pouring sweat, had reached half way. Nothing had happened but Jonathan read correctly every sign that indicated the presence of terrorists. Not a bird moved nor sang whilst the very air seemed still and heavy. Even the insects were noticeably silenced. The large blue and orange - headed lizards which always frequented all such granite boulders and rocks because they loved to be on them basking in the sunshine, were conspicuously absent. Nature itself screamed out that danger was lurking! But where?

"That's strange," Jonathan thought as he sent four more men. Nothing happened - they reached mid-point as the first four attained the far side of the valley. Not a single shot had been fired. Not even the bushes had been stirred.

"Let's go then," ordered Jonathan, "but caution! I don't like this." There was no evidence of movement, no sign of life. Everything was abnormally still: in fact as still as stone. He knew in his bones the terrs were around but where? Where? Why were they not engaging? The valley was perfect for an ambush and the terrs would have had an advantage though there was plenty of cover for his men.

Suddenly as Jonathan was into the valley an incredible peace descended on him. "This is odd," he thought, "we must be out of the `killing zone.'" Little did he know then, but he was only just entering the "killing zone." But, absolutely nothing happened. It was a unique experience which troubled Jonathan for days. Why had the terrs not attacked them? They had to have been around but what had prevented them. It must have been the Lord Jonathan was convinced but he longed to know details. Indeed he would. They passed through the valley and surrounded the village. Nothing and nobody was present. Even the dogs were gone. Unfinished sadza (Staple food of corn meal boiled with water) lay in the pots from the morning breakfast. The village had departed in haste. Jonathan was anxious. It was unexplainable. Nothing fitted a pattern. Nothing pieced together. The terrs must have known he'd follow. Why hadn't they ambushed?

Jonathan was angry as their sweep in a large circle revealed nothing. They had one of his men and they were going to pay. He didn't want to imagine what they were doing to Kizito and blocked the thoughts from his mind.

They returned to base that evening rather deflated after such a build up. There were plenty of prisoners including the treacherous Mai Chitonga. He hated to think what the men would do to her. Jonathan went straight to his office. He worked late into the night compiling a report with all the evidence. He would request the D.C. and even Provincial Commissioner to chopper out and assess the situation. The army must move in. They did and in time Jonathan moved out. He'd done his part. He'd found a major route, major supply area and several large gangs of terrorists.

Jonathan was convinced that the notorious Kufa Ufulu was in charge of the area from the terrorist's aspect. He had worked long enough to identify Ufulu's signs. He left his trademark identifying him himself as he went. His evil and fear had oozed into every home and village anesthetizing the people. They were so bound by their traditions and the dread of ancestral spirits that they dare not oppose or even speak badly of Ufulu for fear that he would know. Torture, death and destruction had left its trail far and wide across Marange. Though Jonathan had fought an incredible battle to win the hearts and minds of the people and to sow Jesus into their lives, he knew that under the prevailing conditions, he had lost. Darkness reigned over Africa. It was that darkness veiling the minds and hearts of a vast continent that kept them prisoners and slaves to the tyranny not of colonial rule but of supernatural powers.

But Jonathan was convinced beyond doubt that those who walked in gross darkness would see a great Light. Africa's day was still coming.

CHAPTER FOUR

AMNESTY

It had been almost a year since joining Internal Affairs. Jonathan had seen much action but was beginning to get restless. The war was hotting up. Terrorists were being slaughtered daily but security force casualties and deaths were mounting. Jonathan was heading up Zimunya Tribal Trust Land. Continuously on the field, the war was getting to him: it was really the inability to reach the unseen enemy which frustrated him most. The danger was nothing with the Lord by his side but none of that was the cause of his restlessness. It was the workings and mechanics of the Holy Spirit leading him out to take him into God's vineyards which were stirring in Jonathan to make him dissatisfied.

He had been assigned to write brochures countering the Marxist propaganda of the terrs. The government had decided on a national leaflet drop to coincide with a soon-coming amnesty for any terr who surrendered. This excited Jonathan as he could use what he had learned at university. All those hours of study were paying off and he knew the Marxist Dialectic well. He could effectively counter it. How his liberal friends would be gnashing their teeth if they knew how he was using that political science. He laughed as he wrote. "Get 'em, get 'em, get 'em," he shouted.

The base was a new site and the living quarters were crude until a proper unit could be built. Jonathan's bathroom consisted of a canvas bath out back surrounded by a thatched wall. It was open to the stars. Not a pleasant place to bathe during icy winter weather or when it drizzled. Needless to say, there was no lounging in the bath. The water was boiled in a forty-four gallon drum over an open fire - a primitive affair. A.D.F. were building a barracks, offices and staff quarters but not Rusty this time! He was still hospitalized. The raison d'etre for this camp was to gather logistics and maintain a presence along a road which led to a major farming area called Burma Valley because of its dense equatorial forest cover which reminded some of the original farmers who had fought there, of Burma. The valley was rich in tobacco, cotton, bananas and citrus crops much of it for export. This made Burma Valley important to the agro industry. The camp was at the foothills of the Vumba mountains which were soon to become world famous. These mountains border directly on Mocambique. The mountains were a paradise of coffee farms, plantations, nature reserves and gardens: excellent cover and provision for the terrs.

The Vumba was majestic and revealed the great glory of God especially in the African dawn. Waterfalls cascaded down, at times lost in the luxuriant growth only to spring to life again further down the slopes. There were pools that looked like liquid glass, that spoke of the serenity and peace of Jesus in a chaotic world. Gazing into the pools Jonathan could feel that river of life springing up from deep within. He'd often resort to a pool for quiet meditation or singing in tongues to the praise and glory of the Giver of Life. Of course there could be terrs around but He who had kept him was well able to overshadow as He was being praised. Jonathan was one who had come to trust; trust simply in the ability of God. That trust grew out of love. Jesus was more than a Savior; He had become a real friend. His spirit would soar to the heights with the eagles as he worshipped with songs he composed by the Spirit:

> Lord You are the pearl of greatest price
> The precious Holy God of sacrifice
> You're the One who died to set me free
> I come now Lord to worship Thee.
>
> You are my reason for living
> You are the Jewel of my life
> Unto You now, all I'm giving
> You're the Way, the Truth and Life.

What a peace and joy the beauty of Jesus provided in the midst of turmoil and strife. It was the calm assurance of one securely grounded on the Rock of Ages which spoke so much to the men.

One day as Jonathan was working, Sgt. Khami who had stayed with him during the move, knocked at the door. "Sir, there's a woman to see you outside. She's the mother of Felix who worked for boss Tony." Tony was a young Internal Affairs Cadet whose life consisted only of wine, women and song. Sadly he had taught his young batman that riotous life. Tony had gone on a course and

Felix had disappeared during his absence. "Show her in Khami." The woman came to the porch. She looked old but was only in her early '30's. She'd probably already born eight or ten children and was worn out. "Manheru," she greeted, clapping her hands and sitting on the ground in customary manner. Jonathan was in uniform and a "big boss" so it would be very rude to shake his hand.

"Manheru, manheru." Jonathan replied.

She began speaking, shaking her head and tutting as she did. Felix was her eldest son and right at that moment he was lying dying at their home some twenty-five miles away in the bush. He was sending his mother to see "Bwana Jonathan" because he'd watched the Bwana so much and knew him to be a "Man of God." "Now," he'd said to his mother, "go to the camp and ask Bwana Jonathan to pray for me and I will recover and not die."

"You mean I must go to him," translated Khami for Jonathan.

"Aikona (no)," the woman said emphatically. "Just pray here now. Felix is very, very sick but said he will be well if the Bwana pray for him."

"Let us pray then," said Jonathan bowing his head. His first silent prayer was, "Lord use this on Khami." Jonathan prayed compassionately for Felix and also laid his hand on the mother and prayed for her. With that, the woman said a simple, "Tatenda (thank you)," and left.

Felix returned a week later. His face was radiant as an angel and he was a changed man. About the time Jonathan prayed Felix had a full vision of Jesus. So white and shining was He that at first Felix was terrified. But Jesus had opened his arms and said, "Come to Me Felix, ye that labor and are heavy laden." With that Felix had surrendered his life and was healed. The proof of the vision was that Felix had never read the Bible nor heard the Scripture which Jesus had spoken but could quote it perfectly. How he rejoiced when Jonathan showed it to him in the Word. His testimony and changed life sent a shock wave through Khami and some other men. When Jonathan shared the Bible with the men at night he noticed for the first time that Khami would creep within hearing distance. He always pretended to be busy with something else, but his heart had been pricked. A couple of days after Tony returned, Felix ran away again. He clear disappeared one night. It would be three years before Jonathan would meet him again.

There was a growing desire in Jonathan's heart to begin mission work. So many multitudes needed to be reached. The tribal natives were receiving Marxist indoctrination. Most of the terrorists had come from traditional mission schools. Where was the preaching of the true Gospel? Where was a burning love for Jesus that would outweigh the fire of revolution that raged in hearts? It was only the Gospel which could turn men's hearts and could change lives. The restlessness which he was feeling was the prompting of the Spirit. It was time to be moving on. Jonathan knew that an effective door would open. He was not anxious. He would wait and spend that waiting giving glory to God.

It was an early August evening in 1976. Jonathan had just completed writing his last leaflet. The amnesty would be announced in the middle of the month and become effective in September. He was pleased with the work. Charles was dozing by the old wood stove. "Bath time, Charles!" Jonathan ordered. "Take out the paraffin (kerosene) lantern but keep it very low just in case." Jonathan was used to working with dimmed lights at night and from a distance the small cottage looked as if in darkness. There should be no indicator on to which the terrorists could zero their mortars or rockets. Caution was always critical. He stepped into the canvas tub and sat down with knees up to his chin and water half way up his thighs. He soaped down. Suddenly that which he feared came to pass. A violent swish of air and an explosion twenty yards away sent shrapnel and debris flying in all directions. He rolled out of the bath and grabbed for his towel and sandals. In the process the bath overturned swamping the lantern and plunging everything into darkness. He lunged for his rifle (the rule was that rifle even went to the bathroom with one) and darted for a bunker in the direction of the firing. RPD's were rattling off outside the fence and RPG7 rockets were whistling through the air and exploding somewhere but Jonathan didn't see or bother where. There was a mightily explosion and "swoosh" close to him. He felt a violent force hit his hand and his finger go numb. "I've lost it," he panicked, "lost my finger". He felt for blood and waited for the aching pain. There was nothing. But, he'd lost something else too. His towel had fallen off. There was no time to retrieve it. "O God," he groaned, "I always wanted to die naked." He heard God chuckle, "Naked you came and naked you go...."

He laughed, "What a sense of humor you have Lord." "O for a towel," cried Jonathan as he fired his way toward the fence and a bunker. There was tracer from all positions but he was NOT going to crawl to the fence this time! That could be more dangerous than a bullet. His men were so dismayed at his naked form shining white in the dark that they stopped firing.

"What are you looking at? Shoot!" he shouted. All Jonathan could see were the whites of their eyes as big as saucers. Jonathan was at least grateful there was no bright moon.

The attack had no sooner ended than his men took off running. "False modesty," sighed Jonathan. He knew how the natives always crept down to the river to peep at any white person bathing. They were fascinated...did they look the same....were they angels....What? It seemed seconds and Charles arrived with pants and trousers. "Prepare my bath Charles."

"Again?" The dismay was funny because Charles really expected another attack if Jonathan bathed again. "They've gone Charles. It's okay." Slipping on his trousers he went to finish his bath. By the light of the lantern, which Charles had retrieved from the mud and lighted, he saw the onyx stone on his ring was completely cracked. No wonder - what an escape! Some years later he would have another miraculous escape from shrapnel. Jonathan still has the ring as evidence of God's power to keep safe his people.

Following that latest incident it was decided to mine detect the road daily. A "Freddie Flintstone" type vehicle arrived. It looked like a small version of Leopard with similar steel plating but was much lighter. Added to that it had only two large cylindrical wheels - one front and back. The "wheels" were about seven to eight feet wide. The engineering behind the vehicle was that the dissipated weight would be such as not to detonate a mine. It worked perfectly and Jonathan never heard of a "Pukie" (the name of a type of night ape which sees well in the dark) as it was called, ever detonating a mine. Inside the cab was sophisticated detection equipment. The vehicle could move quickly. Any metal object - even the smallest piece of tin, would set the alarm buzzing. The engineers would move in to defuse a mine when detected. And so, with fanfare the engineers arrived at the camp. The engineer-in-charge was a young swaggering officer, a real Casanova type who cleared the road each morning and spent the rest of the day sun bathing, showing off his muscular body and reading cheap, trashy novels.

One evening some of the cadets arrived with a big cake tin. Inside was a note, "Got Ya!" and some Mexican-type chilies. The tin was

put in a plastic bag hanging from which were numerous colored wires. They wanted to sneak outside the fence and plant the tin for "cass boy" as he was nicknamed. Next morning as "cass boy" swaggered to his vehicle, the whole camp moved to the fence to watch. If he hadn't been so full of self-importance he'd have noticed and suspected something. The "pukie" sped off. About a hundred feet from the gate it came to a grinding halt. Reverse. Stop. "Hey you guys," he shouted, "there's a Lima Mike here." He carefully laid his cordite and blew away the surface soil. "My, my, my, my! my! What's it Cass?" the chorus shouted. "This is a new one." He went into some long description of the latest Czechoslovakian innovation but added for heroism, "it has to be triple boosted." Everybody was laughing quietly and comments began to fly, "This one got you Cass...."
"Too big for ya big boy..." "Watch ya front...."
"Don't spoil ya face..." He was too full of himself to realize he was being "had" and the sweat was already appearing on his forehead. Jonathan, followed by some of the cadets, ventured out the gate. They all stood around as "Cass" rattled off again the technicalities of the mine. "Well, diffuse it then Cass," someone shouted.
"Everybody stand back now." He knelt gingerly wiping round and round but the wires had really confused him. The sweat was now pouring off his face and his shirt was soaked. Tony stepped forward and grabbing a wire yanked it saying, "What's this?"
There was a yell from Cass as he went diving across the road into the water ditch. He covered his head. He lay for a few seconds before realizing there'd been no explosion. "You ... ass" he screamed. "You could have killed us all." The rest of the group was standing by the road. His rage set the cue for laughter which up to then was being stifled. Men were doubled with laughter as tears poured from many an eye but still Cass did not realize that he had been set up for a fall. "Stand back now and quit laughing. It's not... funny." This is serious stuff. There's never been a mine like this in the country...."
"We believe you...,"
"Cool Cass...,"
"Get her boy...,"
"Go for it...,"
"We know you can do it...."
Again he was kneeling, and gushing sweat. He didn't know where to begin. Everyone was splitting with laughter when a cadet

walked up and said, "I'll show you Cass." He grabbed the plastic bag and dragged the tin from the hole. In one move, Cass was in the ditch again, lying face down with hands covering his head. The cadet walked and stood over him holding the tin. As Cass got up shaking and dusting himself off he was handed the tin.... Nobody heard his swearing and shouting beneath the laughter.

It was a week later that Jonathan received a disturbing report. The army had intercepted a large group of gandangas. Over thirty had been killed, one of whom was a political commissar. In his diary was a report for "May Day," - "Captured one Ground Security officer in Maranke Tribal Trust Land. Name - Kizito. May 8th.: Too many helicopters and army. Moving base. Prisoner tied to tree and shot. Left for hyenas."

"Too, too bad," sighed Jonathan choked up. He thought for a while of all the fun they had enjoyed as well as the action. He left a wife and two small children. Jonathan would visit them when in town. He sent for Khami to tell him the sad news. Though unspoken, they had all hoped that Kizito would make it, would escape.... "Another good man gone," Jonathan said.

The amnesty as announced took effect in September. Life continued normally on base without any further major incidents. Jonathan had made a decision under direction of the Holy Spirit. He had applied for a departmental transfer to take up the offer of a teaching post at the Umtali Boys High School. His main objective was to become fully involved in the ministry of the local Assembly of God to equip him for further service. His soldiering days were by no means ended. His unit was changing. He was about to join the real Army of the Lord under the captaincy of King Jesus. The new appointment was to begin on January 1st, 1977. Before the transfer, God blessed Jonathan with some incredible revelations.

After a couple of months the amnesty, which was well underway, was experiencing a fair amount of success. Terrs were coming in for a variety of reasons. There were whispers that Kufa Ufulu was so ruthless with his own men that some were accepting the amnesty in their desire to escape his lunatic behavior. Others believed that the terrorist armies were losing the war and wanted a change. In actual fact, they were losing the war and hundreds were being killed. Still others were simply tired of fighting and wanted some form of normalcy in their lives. Sometime about mid-November, Jonathan received a message from the Sgt-in-charge at the District Commissioner's officer that he needed to speak. Sgt.

Luke was an old-timer gossip and had been with Internal Affairs for over thirty years. He knew the ins-and-outs of the Ministry and the personal lives of everyone in Umtali District. Any scandal or gossip and Luke knew all the details. If he liked one, he was a wealth of information otherwise he could be very difficult and unco-operative. His eyes and ears were everywhere in the form of every District Assistant, corporal and sergeant as well as the clerks who were under his command. Jonathan knew that he was aware of most of what was contained in the "Top Secret" files though he had never been cleared for Top Secret rating. The "tea boys" would overhear the "Madames" talking or "see" on the District Commissioner's desk. Every bit of information was reported directly to Luke. His system was typically African but very effective and very detailed.

"Sir, about one week ago they bring a gandanga here," he began as they sat in the shade of a large flowering red flamboyant tree. "They call the court interpreter - he's my friend."

"Yes, like everyone, Luke!" They laughed together knowing full well what Jonathan meant.

"Well sir, this gandanga he surrendered. He say he tired of fighting but very afraid 'cos Kufa Ufulu want to kill him so he run away." Luke paused for effect and Jonathan played along. "He was with the 'spirit of death? Go on. Go on, Luke."

"He tell so much about Ufulu: how he train in Czechoslovakia, Yugoslavia, East Germany and Russia. He come back to Mocambique and enter Rhodesia. Surely that one is devil. He drink a white soldier's blood. He take too much medicine. He visit 'ngas (witch doctors). He's a animal. The gandanga say he rape too much and use bayonet on women with baby."

"You mean ripping them open?"

Luke nodded. "He cut off lips and tongue out of people who didn't talk. That gandanga seen him eat people, even testicles of men."

"What!" exclaimed Jonathan. But he knew under witchcraft they were able to do anything. Luke paused again for effect. "Yes, Luke, what else?" He put red-hot stick up people's behind and too, too many other things. People very, very afraid of him 'cos every time he escape security force. They say he has spirit of the M'buya and nobody can kill him. He has power over white men because he drink blood and eat flesh of man."

"I know Luke, he escaped me. But it's really because you blacks are too superstitious and are afraid of killing him. Where's that gandanga now? I'd like to meet him."

"He gone to Salisbury."

"Well Luke that confirms all the info we have about him. Thank you for telling me." Luke cleared his throat somewhat nervously.

"But Sir...."

"What Luke?"

"That gandanga say that Ufulu specially want to kill you himself better all capture you, Sir. Sir must be very careful. He want you too bad."

"I want him too bad too Luke. But why me?" Luke coughed. "Because you have too much power. He hate you for that. He know your name and tell all gandangas to capture you alive. Kufa Ufulu want to prove that his power is greater than yours.

"Then he will have to fight Jesus," laughed Jonathan standing up to go. "It's the darkness of the devil versus the light of God." Luke grabbed Jonathan's arm and pulled him down again. Then he furtively looked around and began to whisper.

"But Sir, they was in Maranke. They specially planted that mine for you - you know the one that Mr. Rusty hit. That night when you pass they not expected you to come. They run from the store but too late. You were gone!"

"What!" said Jonathan. "That terr was there?"

"Yes Sir with Ufulu too," exclaimed Luke knowingly.

"With Ufulu?" breathed Jonathan with a whistle.

"Yes, Sir. And with Ufulu. So next' day when Mr. Rusty hit that mine they not capture him 'cos they wanting you too bad. Ufulu say, `This my chance. That Jonathan will come and we will ambush.' But Sir, as you arrive the helicopters came. They heard them and run. Ufulu was too furious. He said, `tonight we get him at base.' They give to one woman who was drawing water at the borehole near the fence a wire to put on the fence...."

"I knew it, I knew it! So it was Ufulu! I smelled his work out there. It had to be him."

"They knowed your house, Sir, and seed you run out and fall. Ufulu thought you was dead. Nex' day it reported him that you alive. He's so angry he beat his men an' killed villagers."

"Wow! Did he say anything about Kizito and what happened?"

"That gandanga sayed that they reach the base after Kizito captured. But his friend was in the mountains to ambush you when you pass. They were too happy to shoot you. They seed you come but then sayed they was too scared to shoot. They become like stones. They can't move."

"Why?"

"Because, they seed too many big white, very white soldiers with very shiny uniform. Not any one gandanga was able to fire. They very afraid and after you passed by they run and hide. Great, great fear, Sir. They refuse to tell Ufulu about that for fear of what he will do to them."

"What a Mighty God," was all Jonathan could whisper. "Those were angels Luke, you'd better believe."

"I believing, Sir. I knowed all about you."

"Thank you Luke," as Jonathan slipped him a ten dollar note. "It's wonderful that God reveals those things to His glory. No wonder the peace descended in that valley. He was there and there was nothing anyone could do. How true that "no weapon formed against us can prosper."

CHAPTER FIVE

SCHOOL

Jonathan was not new to teaching. He had taught a year at a private college, St. Stephens after leaving university and prior to going to England. But the College had closed as a result of war. The next years were the Holy Spirit's final preparation to launch Jonathan into ministry. The school was situated on a hill in the northern suburbs overlooking the town. And yes, it was situated right on the Mocambican border. From the top floor of a modern glass and steel hostel block, home to Jonathan for two years, he could see the huge double security fence that ran along the border with mine fields between. The hostel was a perfect target for the enemy. Nobody could escape the war and its effects.

Jonathan quickly threw himself with zeal into his teaching, hostel duties, sporting activities but most of all into the spiritual life of both the local church and his students. Umtali was the fourth largest city of Rhodesia and capital of the eastern province. Spiritually it was a tough town. Umtali was always a stepping-stone to one of the three much larger centers of the country. People were migratory and few, no matter in what areas of life they were, came to settle. At one time it was the bustling tourist eastern gateway to the popular Mocambican holiday resorts. But, since Portugal had given independence to Mocambique under its wicked communist regime, the borders were closed and sealed. Now the two countries were in a state of undeclared war and Mocambique gave safe sanctuary to the multitudes of terrorists who came across the border.

They were days of severe petrol (gas) rationing in Rhodesia and because Jonathan lived at his place of work he received the basic ration of only six units-which amounted to eight-gallons per month. There was certainly no place for unnecessary driving but the Lord always provided abundantly in the ministry work. When Jonathan assumed the responsibility of lay preaching, his ration increased to the grand sum of fourteen units. Wow! That was almost half-a-gallon of fuel per day. Consequently, Jonathan's burnt orange car always remained in the garage during the week. This, together with his red hair, his preaching and his no nonsense discipline quickly earned him the popular title of "Red Rev." They were days when lady teachers far outnumbered their male counterparts who had all gone to war. Teenage boys needed strong men and they responded quickly to Jonathan. There were always groups of young boys around him talking, laughing and listening. He would take them on hikes up the mountains behind the school and listen to their problems and young teenage heartaches. Many of the children came from broken homes and had the added hang-ups of rejection compounded by war and the military life which invaded every family.

He was master-in-charge of swimming and water polo and spent much time at the pool coaching. Every second weekend there was a match or tournament. They alternated home and away so at least once a month he traveled with his team the hundred and fifty miles to Salisbury or further which meant leaving on Friday and returning Sunday. The bus journeys were very tiresome unless he drove but he enjoyed it because the boys enjoyed it. Playing "away" games always meant special treats especially for those in the hostels. Once a month he also had weekend hostel duty which required him to oversee the hostel from Friday morning until Monday morning. At those times he would hire a film for the boys and generally allow them as much freedom as possible.

Jonathan struck up a rich and immediate friendship with the cook matron who was a saint. She was an old time Rhodesian farmer her husband having ditched her twenty years previously. She had raised two fine sons and a lovely daughter and retired from farming comfortably off. She took the despised post of "cook matron" because she so badly wanted to do something for Jesus. And so, there she was immersed in the spoiling of young boys and talking to them about Jesus. Jonathan and Bess made a strong team and before long they had impacted the hostel with the Gospel. Their cars became regular taxis ferrying boys to Gospel meetings and church services as often as possible. The joy of seeing dozens of boys won to Jesus in a hostel of one hundred and twenty was thrilling and satisfying to Bess. She endured the continuous venom of the hostel superintendent who loathed Christians as did the other matrons. Matrons were a breed on their own: usually frustrated old cantankerous ladies who could form a very strong "gaggle" and oust anyone who would not conform. Bess would not conform to their ways. She didn't need the job but was efficient and an excellent cook.

One morning, Bess collapsed with a major heart attack. The ambulance arrived and rushed her to hospital. One of the other old matrons sent a schoolboy with an inexplicit message simply saying, "Mrs. Wills, would like to see you." She was always doing it so Jonathan didn't hurry. At breakfast he was in a jovial mood. His colleague asked him,

"What are you so happy about?"

"Why, it's a lovely day..."

"Don't you know about Bess?"

"What about her?"

"She collapsed outside the kitchen this morning with a major heart attack and was rushed to hospital."

"Supervise my class for me, Margie. Tell the head I'll be back as soon as possible." The Red Rev. rushed off to the hospital to find Bess in intensive care and wired up to all kinds of monitors. As he arrived the oscilloscope was already showing a straight line and beeping. The nurse shook her head, "I'm sorry, she's been gone quite a while."

"Impossible!" Jonathan blurted, "We had a deal. Would you give me one minute alone with her? I'd like to pray. Please!" The nurse slipped out. There was no heartbeat or breath. Bess and Jonathan had always joked about who would get to heaven first. "Bess," Jonathan shouted the command, "you're not going yet. There's work to do. Now in the name of Jesus of Nazareth, come back and rise." At that instant her heart began to beat ever so faintly and gradually gained strength as the minutes passed. The nurse could not believe and fled to call the doctor. "She'll not live," he insisted, "call her family."

"O yes doctor, Jesus has restored her life. She will live." And so she did, to continue her work in the hostel and later in Ireland to where she retired.

More and more boys started attending church, getting saved and receiving the Baptism of the Holy Spirit. Soon the school was abuzz and it caused no small amount of stir amongst the staff that everybody was getting "religious." The headmaster summoned Jonathan, "You will stop talking this religion and indoctrinating the students...."

"Sir," said Jonathan, "may I ask, can you fault my teaching?"

"Well no, your results are excellent but..."

"Sir, if your other teachers discuss rugby and movies and discotheques; I discuss not religion but Jesus."

"It's got to stop..."

"I cannot Sir. You'll have to decide what to do with me...."

That terminated the conversation and Jonathan became the "Pied Piper" to so many students. Wherever he went crowds of boys were always waiting to ask questions, help in any way possible or just wanted a smile or acknowledgment. Jonathan became a teacher-hero. He loved the boys but would take no nonsense. "It is Christ in me they loved," he declared in later years, "because really in the natural I was tough. The boys came to him with their problems and tears, with their victories and joys and with their questions about life. Many were farmers' children - especially the hostel students - with fears and worries about their families and friends on their lonely farmstead. It provided perfect opportunities for Jonathan to minister the love and victory of a risen and living Savior. The hostel was turned around as dozens upon dozens of boys came through to a saving knowledge of Jesus. The mini revival continued. Meantime at church, God was visiting with wave upon wave of His glory. There were no great crowds, no spectacular miracles, no dynamic preaching. But there were some incredible ingredients which brought God's awesome presence. There was such a love for God as to stir hearts to do anything. Together with that love was a compassion for the lost and a humble dependence upon God to do everything. Oh indeed, it was days of heaven on earth. Such peace and joy and the presence of the Holy Spirit pervaded the church that people would just sit in the building for the refreshment of His presence. God would explode upon every meeting and there was life. This was prelude to a much greater work which was to be like living in the Book of Acts all over again. The net results were that there came a burden to reach the lost. Despite the dangers of the war teams went forth preaching and teaching and establishing Bible studies throughout Manicaland Province. In particular, Jonathan carried two major burdens. The one was to reach the multitudes in the Tribal Trust Lands, not only where he had worked, but elsewhere. No mission work was being done among the natives. It was a vast untapped field of precious souls but there were no harvesters to put in the sickle and reap. The second burden was to reach neighboring Mocambique. Since the earliest Portuguese days of 1492 Mocambique had been under the heel of Rome. There was never freedom to preach the Gospel. Now the country had fallen under the iron boot of communism and enslaved to the masters in Moscow and East Berlin. The church that had existed was being violently persecuted. Buildings were closed or commandeered for other purposes. Pastors were imprisoned, tortured and killed. Congregations were sent to slave labor camps. But as so often with men under persecution, they began to cry out to God and a vibrant underground church began to take root and flourish.

Jonathan strengthened the links with Richard Wurmbrand and established contacts with Open Doors and Brother Andrew. He began to smuggle Bibles into Mocambique through native couriers. The work was exceptionally dangerous for those brave men, many of whom died and joined the ranks of God's noble martyr band. They had to make secret contact across the border. Then there was the problem of the communist FRELIMO government forces of Mocambique to be avoided and even the Rhodesian forces. Freedom of movement across the border was stopped. If the couriers could successfully escape all those dangers, there were finally the minefields. But there are no limits to what men will do when really thirsty for God's Word. And so secretly, Bibles began to cross as well as brochures on "Christ's answer to Marx." It would be five years of this clandestine work before Jonathan could cross himself but this small sideline ministry developed into something much larger with hundreds of Bibles crossing to Mocambique each month. A decade later, they would themselves purchase and take into Mocambique over 100,000 Bibles in two years - over 1,000 Bibles per week. Never had Mocambique been so bombarded with God's Word in the nearly 500 years that Mocambique had been a colony of Portugal. Evangelism had always been forbidden during that long era.

Ministry was started amongst farm laborers and Jonathan began to train natives for the ministry while training himself. An evangelistic team complete with singers and musicians would travel to remote areas for the purpose of the Gospel. The fearlessness, which the Spirit instilled in Jonathan, was contagious. In their love for God, the band saw His mightiness, His ability and His salvation rather than the war circumstances. Throughout the remaining three years of war not a single worker was killed, captured or even slightly injured. The God of the Old Testament who could keep the Hebrew boys from even smelling of smoke in the furnace proved Himself able and willing again and again.

"And there was a certain widow in the church..." Maggie was to Jonathan what Mary had been to Jesus. She was born to serve; a veritable saint who never became upset or angry though she endured incredible trials. Maggie was a backbone of the church: not only in labor but in support as well. She was just the kind of strength and encouragement a young minister needed. Mixed with all those remarkable characteristics she had the most incredible sense of humor. She joined the "taxi rank" along with Bess. Her little Datsun 120Y would ooze kids out of every available space. She would cook and fetch and carry and buy... and was so hospitable.

The church was given an old 1958 Dodge pickup. They built a canopy for her and she became the "Hallelujah Wagon." They were off with Maggie's Taxi to do some Gospel meetings but as usual, Africa has no time frame. The team arrived in dribs and drabs resulting in a very late start. As they neared their destination it was already dark. The lights of the Dodge were not good and it was raining. Suddenly, an ox crossed the road.... "Good-bye ox!" The Dodge hit it and it flew into the air.

"O my Lord, save Maggie, she's behind!" was all Jonathan groaned as he had visions of ox coming down on the Datsun "taxi". Maggie had seen and swerved. The ox was dead. The Dodge made of solid steel, was hardly dented and Maggie was fine.

It was August of 1978 when Jonathan was officially ordained. He had one term left at school and it was the summer vacation. The hostel was empty - boys had gone, matrons had gone and even the superintendent had left. One evening, Jonathan had an unexpected visitor. Everything was still and dark. He sat downstairs in the staff room. Suddenly there was a violent wind: it caused the door to slam so hard that the entire building shook.

Then, Satan himself was in the room. Jonathan's hair was standing up; the most incredible, frightening evil was all around. He'd sensed the same experience when dealing with the terrs only this time it was on a far greater scale. Instinctively he wanted to run. He couldn't see any form but satan was there and laughing.

"What d'you want?' he addressed the unseen being.

"Just visiting," he heard the distinctive reply.

"Well, in Jesus name, get out!" With that Jonathan opened the door and marched up to his room. The corridors echoed and satan followed. As he reached the top floor Jonathan turned on the stairs and commanded:

"Now leave in the name of Jesus." The louver windows rattled and with a shriek he was gone. Ten years later satan visited again and told Jonathan he would destroy him which he really tried to do but God who is greater has ever been faithful not only to sustain, but to increase.

The visit of satan was prelude to two things. A farmer in the church was notorious for his ability to "water divine". Jonathan had strongly disapproved of this method of finding water, citing that it was demonic. Nik was an old weathered Rhodesian farmer who took pride in his skills and knowledge. He was an astute cattle farmer who knew the ways of the bushveld having grown up in the saddle. He had recently surrendered to Christ which was a major event in his life. Step by step, Nik was being broken down to trust the Lord: stripped as only God can do, so as to build a vessel fit for his Master's use. His son-in-law, Pat, was in the police anti-terrorist unit. One afternoon Pat had been driving back to Umtali when he was ambushed by a group of terrs. In his effort to both steer his Landover and fire his rifle he'd over-turned the Landover. Pat was thrown out of the vehicle, which toppled on to his leg pinning him down. The jubilant terrs had rushed from their ambush positions smelling the blood of a white policeman. Pat's leg was trapped and crushed under the weight of the Landover. He couldn't move. The terrs were advancing. He couldn't reach his rifle. He knew he was dead. Suddenly he called out in faith, "Jesus please help me." Pat had recently come to know Jesus in such a personal way that it had brought his whole family to the Lord.

Suddenly the unbelievable happened! Pat saw the Landover being lifted off his leg. It clearly lifted about a foot. Pat dragged out his leg which was burning with fire. The terrs were advancing but not shooting. Pat leaped to his feet and bolted off into the bush. His bones were healed. There was only a flesh wound on his thigh. He ran for his life until his lungs were ready to burst, but he'd escaped and was safe. What a miracle. Such a deliverance melted old Nik.

Jonathan challenged Nik on his divining and very confident, Nik took up the challenge. They walked out into the bush and stood under an old Baobab tree. Nik carried his "wish-bone" divining rod which was smooth and polished with age. It was a perfect Rhodesian setting: the dry bushveld with acacia thorns dotted here-and-there cast pools of shade on the dusty land in the midday heat. The gnarled branches of the huge baobab reached nakedly for the sky. The natives believe that the Baobab was the last tree which God planted. Their story goes that He was so tired that he planted the tree upside down because the trunk and branches look like an enormous root system.

"Lord reveal the truth of this thing," prayed Jonathan simply. Nik lifted his stick. It was still. Nothing happened for a moment. All of a sudden the stick began to dip and rise, dip and rise getting more and more fierce with each oscillation. Soon the stick was dipping and rising with such violence that Nik was being lifted clean off his feet. He couldn't let go of the stick. He was shouting. His veld hat went flying through the air. Then, there was a resounding crack as if a rifle had been fired. The stick, fully two inches in diameter exploded into fragments. Nik collapsed on the ground defeated and exhausted as well as visibly shaken. It was the end of his divining. The power was broken. God had triumphed.

Soon after satan's visit and seemingly coincidentally, school began again and the hostel came under attack. Indeed, missiles began to fall on the entire city. The boys were excited as the siren wailed, the alert button to the police station buzzed and glass shattered all around them. Boys were crawling down the stairs dragging blankets, whispering excitedly and speculating. They had done the drill every term but this was the real thing! How thrilling! They could hear the mighty explosions as missiles shook the whole town. Prefects and teachers took the roll call. Then, amidst fear and excitement the boys jabbered out their endless string of questions.

"Sir, tell us about when you were fighting."

"Was it like this."

"This is scary."

"Don't be a coward!"

"Will we die," came a timid voice that immediately threw Jonathan back to Peter on the mountainside.

"No, no!" said Jonathan yet again with rifle in his hand.

"We're perfectly safe here," except he thought, if we get a direct missile strike. And, that was possible.

"Are you afraid, Sir?"

"No, Duncan, I've seen worse but Jesus always looks after us."

"Will they come to the fence and attack?"

"No Brett, soon our air force will come, you'll see."

It was not long before the air force did arrive, screaming into Mocambique - Phantoms and Hunters, followed by Canberra bombers. The whole earth shook as the bombs fell and the air to ground rockets swooshed to their targets. The boys gave a resounding cheer. Even from the safe place, they could see the sky light up with the explosions. The attacks and counter-attacks ran nightly for a week. Several missiles, which fell on the city, did not even explode. The most incredible thing was that in all the activity not a single person was injured let alone killed and no damage was inflicted on any buildings. Every missile had landed on a vacant lot or in a street.

God had heard and been faithful to the consistent intercessions of His people. The Holy Spirit had sent out warning signals and for almost a year Jonathan had taught and led one group of powerful intercessors. They had saturated the city with prayer. There were several reported cases of angelic sightings. Ironically in one of the eastern suburbs of the city there was a large kopje (hill) upon which stood an enormous stone cross commemorating the many Rhodesian soldiers both black and white who had given their lives in Burma. It was a landmark which the citizens and intelligence knew was used as a direction finder for the enemy. Another team of intercessors had met weekly on "Cross Kopje" for some considerable time to pray for the protection of Umtali which nestles under the shadow of the huge stone cross. There were efforts by a few to remove the cross but the cross remained to the testimony of God's power: the citizens refused to have their landmark dismantled by the armed forces; they'd rather have the bombs and God's protecting hand as he covered the city with His precious blood so that the destroyer could not come in, than have that cross removed.

What deliverance and victory for those who will trust neither in chariots nor horses but in the mighty name of the Lord Sabaoth. In those days there arose such a vast volume of prayers to God with strong pleadings that God indeed heard the cry of His people. Not a single citizen ever died in the town as God overshadowed with His Mighty wings.

CHAPTER SIX

ELIM: LORD, WE DON'T UNDERSTAND BUT WE TRUST

Sir, there's a lady on the 'phone who says it's very urgent." It was 5.30 a.m. Saturday morning and not a time to be disturbed by anyone (but, Jonathan was on weekend hostel duty).
"Thank you Wilson," he smiled as he ran downstairs.
"Hello, Jonathan. Jonathan, listen quickly, I don't have much time. I'm on duty at the exchange," Elizabeth spoke in hushed tones. "I've just switched a call from Vumba. I wanted you to be the first to know. The missionaries - they were all massacred last night."
"What?" gasped Jonathan. He felt as though he'd just been kicked in the stomach and as if ice cold water had been poured all over him.
"Don't go up there Jonathan. The caller from the school says it's so bad, the bodies are so mutilated.... Please don't go.... The army's on their way now."
"Wendy?"
"She's dead Jonathan. I'm so sorry. One woman is alive but she's so butchered she cannot possibly live. They were all butchered with axes."
"Oh God no!" Jonathan groaned in agony as his whole being went numb.
"Thank you Liz," he mumbled as he put down the receiver.
He staggered back to his room, sat down on the bed and wept. "Precious, sweet, dear Wendy - gone!"
Jonathan's first experience with Elim had been through a long time friend of Bess's, Joan Cordell. Every so often, Joan would travel all the way from Katerere in North Inyanga Tribal Trust Land in her little Austin to "get away from it all." Joan was an accomplished organist and missionary teacher of decades and on many varied mission fields of the world. She would sit for hours and play at the organ in church as she said that the peace and love simply revived her so much that the very dangerous journey across mine-infested roads was worth it. Elim mission was a

school/hospital complex founded through the vision, faith and hard labors of a friend of Jonathan's. A native servant who had worked for years in Salisbury became saved and gloriously filled with the Holy Spirit. Such was the burden to share the message of love with his people that he resigned his job and returned to Katerere, his traditional home. The native servant was industrious and faithful in sharing the Gospel and many in the tribe received Christ. The man began to speak with the chief about a mission and to his dismay a Roman priest arrived one day also requesting land on which to build a mission. The man pleaded with the chief that his missionaries were coming and to give him time. Chief Katerere agreed that, if within six months his missionaries did not come, land would indeed be given to the Romans for a mission station.

The native servant had no missionaries but he had a BIG GOD and believed that God would hear His cry. And so, he began to pray with great searchings and rendings of his heart that God would send a missionary of His kind. As the native touched the heart of God in his pleadings, God began to stir up the saintly missionary Idris Davies in Salisbury. Like Abraham of old, he set out with a friend in his 1937 vehicle - you know the type where the battery was carried in a wire cage under the chassis. He knew not where he was going but was daily led by the Spirit as he journeyed to the east and then north through the Nyanga mountains then on into the rolling plains of Katerere.

It was late one night that Idris arrived on the outskirts of a large village which was obviously the headquarters of a tribal chief. Not wishing to disturb the village, the men parked their vehicle set up their canvas cots and fell into a goodly sleep. They were suddenly awakened in the early hours of the morning by the cries of a native who was speaking in English. "O Lord, today's my last day. Please send the missionaries...." And, there they were in obedient response to the Holy Spirit because of the faithful cries of one believing native. What a mighty God!

Joan shared the incredible stress the missionary staff at Elim was under. They were being regularly visited by the terrorists who demanded medicine and food in exchange for the continued existence of the mission. The staff was horribly caught between the terrorists and the security forces. This situation went on for sometime. One day, Bess came and told Jonathan, "There must be a time when our Christian duty requires us to do something about the terrorists."

"Well, yes Bess, but what are the circumstances?" queried Jonathan.

"I'm talking about Elim. It's really time the security forces became involved up there. That situation cannot continue.... I have to do something." Bess was showing that no nonsense, tough Rhodesian farmer and gold miner character. She had fought many battles in her life and was in a fighting mood.

It was at the beginning of summer 1977 then, that Elim Mission moved into the magnificent Vumba Mountains. They took up abode in the old "Eagle School" which had been an elite private preparatory school. The migratory trip was fraught with danger, trials and heartaches all the way. The leading bus in the convoy detonated a land mine. Many of the students had been killed and many more injured, some seriously.

The peace, serenity and beauty of the Vumba with the dancing mountain streams was a far cry from the hot, dusty plains of north Inyanga with its turmoil and strife. The new term saw the school in fresh surroundings with renewed vigor and hope. And so it was that Jonathan became intimately associated with Elim though not the Eagle School property as he had been accustomed to visiting it - resorting to the site which overlooked Zimunya Tribal Trust Land - for meditation and prayer. The whole place was overgrown and deserted but the buildings were in good condition and Jonathan had a mind to purchase the place for a Bible College one day. He knew the place well and often took selected friends and visitors there to share his dream. Of course it was dangerous. Of course there could be terrorists around but then Umtali was dangerous too.

Wendy Hamilton was a qualified S.R.N. who had been seconded into the teaching department because of a lack of staff. She'd arrived at church one Saturday evening to share in the Lord's Supper and soon struck up a friendship with Jonathan. "Purely platonic," he assured everyone. But Bess was elated because she'd always wanted to see Jonathan "bite the dust" and quickly volunteered her catering services for a wedding.

"You've got it all wrong, Bess," he chided.

"Ha ha! my friend. This old bird might have a scrawny neck and few feathers left but she can fly," she laughed. "You're just a yellow belly."

They always teased each other and Jonathan always asked her,

"Why do you want me to possibly endure the misery you had?"

Everybody always wanted Jonathan to "settle down" but nobody really knew that he had already "settled in" with the Lord and just how intimate and nuts he was about his Savior.

Well, whatever the relationship, he never did reveal to anyone. Suffice it to say they were very good friends which often meant trips to Vumba to fetch Wendy as she had no transport, or to take her some groceries. He also offered to help her with her teaching whenever she needed it. Purely platonic!

A Saturday afternoon would be spent walking in the lovely mountains, singing and sharing the goodness of the Lord in the midst of His perfect creation. Occasionally Jonathan would hint that she needed to be careful and that, in fact, the school was irresponsible not to erect security fences with alarms.

"Wendy, I know the Lord is able. I'm living testimony of that. Look at that base camp down there. That's one place I saw the hand of God protect..." as he pointed out the camp in Zimunya. Things were fine until Jonathan arrived at the Eagle School one winter afternoon in early June 1978. It was cool and the sun was already dipping below the western peaks. As he drove into the school grounds, he knew, knew beyond a shadow of doubt, that the school had been "visited" and that the terrs had just left. He could "smell" them. He was an expert in discerning their whereabouts having been hunted by them as well as hunting them.

"They've been haven't they, Wendy? What do they want? Did you talk to them?" Jonathan demanded.

"No. Some of the boys were spoken to...."

"Has it been reported to the Police?" interrogated Jonathan.

"I...I...I think so, but don't make it hard, Jonathan."

"Hard!" He sternly rebuked. "You don't know what you're up against here. Katerere was tame with what's here." He proceeded to tell her of the "spirit of death," Kufa Ufulu. "You don't know this creature Wendy. He's evil, malicious and out for blood."

Wendy was "living in" for the mission director, Peter Griffiths who was on a year's furlough in Britain. Jonathan remembers well the house. Sometime after the "visit" he arrived again one afternoon and the front door was open. There was a rail along part of the passage leading down a couple of steps into the lounge. Wendy had set a desk against the wall near the steps. As one entered the front door the desk was diagonally to the right perhaps about three paces away. Jonathan stopped and gasped. Another of those movie scenes unrolled before him. He saw Wendy sitting at her desk marking books as a native quietly slipped through the open front door and stabbed her to death. He shared this with her, making her promise from then on that she would keep the door locked.

"You need a pistol, Wendy. Actually, it's time you all got out."

"Please," she would always plead when it came to that subject, "we're having a meeting and some decisions are to be made."

"Not soon enough for me. Do the police really know? I cannot understand why they have not closed you down or at least forced you to fence the place. Why no army presence?" Jonathan was beginning to "suspect" and made a mental note to "ask some questions" and see the police. The following Saturday, Wendy called Jonathan, asking him to fetch her at a home in one of the Umtali suburbs. She was very quiet and upset as they drove to Vumba. Finally she whispered, "We're closing the school. We were informed today at this meeting."

"Good. Leave now or at least tomorrow when I come. Maggie will have you.... You can drive up daily. We'll organize a car for you. "Don't!" was all she said. She was deeply in love with the students, her work, and the school.

Sunday morning Jonathan drove up to Elim again. He was scheduled to preach at the weekly chapel meeting. Most of the staff had stayed over in town with friends. There was a chaotic spirit in the hall. Jonathan was convinced that some terrorists were present in disguise. He preached with all his heart but he felt he was chipping away at an incredible wall of resistance. Finally the break came and the message "took off." Jonathan wove into his message Christ's answer to Marx and ended with a clear challenge to the students to choose between life and death. It was an incredible prophetic challenge.

At the altar appeal, about eighty pupils went forward for Jesus - almost one third of those present. Jonathan was amazed. He and Wendy counseled for a long time. As they were leaving the hall he said to Wendy, "You know what infuriates me about mission schools? They spend all their time giving their kids an academic education without ensuring the eternity of their souls. I cannot believe so many in a mission school have never made a decision for Jesus. The problem is, they have been thoroughly indoctrinated by the terrs." Jonathan didn't expect or elicit a reply. He was righteously angry and indignant and deeply disturbed at the lack of spirituality in the mission.

He had a simple lunch with Wendy and left. He never saw her again. Five nights later the terrible deed was done. The most incredible thing to Jonathan was that the Holy Spirit had not laid a burden on his heart. He was weekend duty master and yet, unlike other times he'd not even thought about Elim or been stirred about the school in the Vumba mountains during that Friday evening. At the very time he was meditating and praying in his study, the evil deed was being perpetrated.

Headlines screamed out to the world:

"ELIM MISSION MASSACRE."

"A band of guerrillas crossed into eastern Rhodesia late last week and laid waste to a British-run missionary outpost in Vumba near the town of Umtali. They slaughtered twelve of the whites including three little girls and a baby.

All had been hideously mutilated - hacked and bayoneted to death, bludgeoned with wooden clubs and rifle butts."

Mrs. Sandra McCann lay with her hand draped over the body of her three-week old baby. The baby's skull appeared to have been crushed."

The mass funeral was a resounding victory for Christ. Even the hardest reporters who flocked in from all over the world were weeping. The funeral ended with a plea to pray for those who had perpetrated the terrible massacre. Jonathan could think only of the "spirit of death" Kufa Ufulu. He alone was capable of such mutilation. What wickedness: no respect for humanity. Only the devil could inspire such deeds in his hatred for the human race especially those who trust in Jesus. The massacre shook the nation and for the first time convinced an unbelieving world that Rhodesians were fighting a war against wicked terrorism. The women's breasts had been cut off; eyes had been gouged out, arms dismembered and everyone sexually mutilated. The tough RLI troops and hardened Selous Scouts had vomited their way through the clean up operations so terrible was the deed. It was Kufa Ufulu, they were his trademarks and Jonathan recognized them. Today a simple stone monument overlooks the site of the school and playing fields which Jonathan knew so well and where he had spent so much time. Inscribed are the simple words: "Lord we do not understand but we trust You."

Elim mission was far from over. The blood of the martyrs *IS* the seed of the church.

CHAPTER SEVEN

BACK TO THE BUSH

And so Jonathan returned to bush life. He lived alone on a remote farm in a tobacco growing community some fifty miles west of Umtali. Actually, his parish became the whole province from the magnificent Inyanga Mountains hugging the Eastern border of Rhodesia to the dry dusty plains of the Sabi Valley. The mountains were cool and exhilarating during the hot summers with their forests of pine and life - gurgling streams and rivers teaming with trout. The Sabi Valley on the other hand, had a wild African charm all of its own: remote, hostile and the Sabi River itself was home to hordes of dreaded crocodiles. It was along the Sabi that a friend of Jonathan established a small experimental fresh - water shrimp farm. One evening he was out hunting with his three Labradors. Suddenly there was a commotion in the bush and without warning a huge crocodile came racing out of the undergrowth catching one of the Labradors with its large tail and flinging it high into the air. As the shrieking animal hit the ground, the crocodile caught it again and flicked him into the air and towards the river. The croc moving with lightening speed and dexterity through the bush finally caught the dog one last time and with great accuracy propelled it into the river. The croc itself took to the water like lightening to seize the poor Labrador as he hit the surface. The whole event took place so quickly that Jim had been unable to shoot at the creature as it moved through the undergrowth.

It is known that crocodiles have a particular fondness for dogs. In the wilds of Africa they can sense when wild dogs are pursuing a buck. The crocodiles will allow the hunted antelope to cross the pond or river and seize the dogs as they follow. Before the crocodile takes its prey, it always sheds copious tears hence the term, "crocodile tears".

Jim was recounting this event to another friend of his who was visiting the Sabi while on honeymoon with his new bride of two days. They were out walking one evening and the bridegroom waded into the shallows of the Sabi River to cool off from the heat. The river was separated into two streams by a large central sandbank. The sun was setting, the doves were cooing in the trees and the "Go-Away" birds were shouting out their warnings to the animals because of the human presence. The birds always warn the animals. Jim's' continuous cautioning of the bridegroom about the crocodiles fell on deaf ears as he waded across to the sandbank. Without indication he dived into the main stream and began swimming to the far bank. Jim fired some warning shots but to no avail. The man was heedless.

Suddenly there was an awful scream. Jim and the new wife stood aghast as they saw the man thrown high into the air. As he hit the water the crocodile had him. Croc and man rolled over and over a few times before disappearing around the bend of the river. The new bride collapsed into a fit of hysteria. Her bridegroom was never seen again.

"It was just as quick as that," said Jim. "Unbelievably frightening. It has given me an even healthier respect for those creatures."

"Yea, they're so evil. I believe them to be corruptions of some other creature," indicated Jonathan to Jim one day. There's a great lesson in all that. Life is so tenuous and without Jesus we're really lost. We can lose our lives so very quickly."

The Sabi Crocs were to be more famous in later days.

It was the last year of war. The words of the Lord, "You will die in the east," rang in his ears but he was not afraid. The task he faced was enormous. There were five "regulars" in his congregation and maybe nine, with visitors. The lady's Bible Study was a little more successful with ten in attendance. There was very little money and he was cast upon the Lord for his all.

"Such fertile training ground," says Jonathan, "to become `fine tuned' to the Holy Spirit. It was the loneliness which was a great trial. I had always been a loner," said Jonathan, "but this was something altogether different. I realized that if I did not conquer this I would never be effective for the Lord. I wrestled and struggled with it for weeks. Oh, I had a good relationship with Jesus but so long as I desired the company of others, or to be active, I had not conquered. Many a young person is defeated by this detail alone and never reaches their full potential or any potential for God because they never conquer loneliness. The matter was settled once and for all one night. I wanted to leap into my car and drive, drive anywhere to anyone but I refrained. I put on a Christian record and began to dance in my enormous lounge. Suddenly the presence of Almighty God so descended and filled that room that I thought I was in heaven. The liquid love of God poured out upon me and filled me until I was compelled to cry, `enough Lord or I die!' The infinite was meeting the finite; the supernatural, the natural; the omnipotent, the feeble. I saw in part the greatness of a Great God and realized, not in word, but in the depths of my soul, that He, God Himself through Jesus, was my reward and my all. He'd won. I'd broken through. From that day I have never suffered a moment's loneliness. He's my delight and total satisfaction as long as I abide in fellowship. God Himself came and filled me in accordance with His Word: `the love of God is shed abroad in our hearts by the Holy Ghost.' (Rom 5:5). I realized that if there was a Baptism into Jesus, a Baptism of the Holy Spirit then there also was a `Baptism of God the Father!' I experienced it that night. God Himself became so real; as real as He had been to Abraham talking as friend to friend.

I was changed. A new dynamism entered my life. If I was radical before now I became 'recklessly abandoned.' I was dying and I didn't realize it. From that moment on, I had a 'ball' with God. Up to then I had seen His grace at work in my life as He kept me, protected me and walked with me. But now, I was working with Him and the results were His. It was His work, His provision and all of Him. A new kind of peace flooded my whole life; a peace that just being in intimate fellowship with God, being conscious of Him moment by moment of each day was the highest calling and total satisfaction. That is true religion.

It did not mean that my activities ceased or grew any less. If anything, I did more because I felt like a walking atom bomb ready to explode. But I was no more 'results anxious.' Who can be when God has become all in all?"

Living alone on the farm proved exciting and a little trying at first. I still had my rifle," declared Jonathan. "A security fence did surround the house but there was no alarm and only one old hand-cranked telephone. The operator was usually sound asleep after 10.00 p.m. (after all, farmers went to bed with the sun) and would have been useless in an emergency."

Jonathan traveled the dusty bush roads with his rifle in the trunk of his little white Isuzu Bellet, 1968 model. A great help it would have been in an ambush but then God was over-shadowing him and he had no doubt on that score. Colleagues in the ministry would rebuke him for "tempting the Lord." Others would laugh, "we're allergic to lead," and call Jonathan "Bellet Bullet" because he was known to drive fast and could "outrun" a bullet.

After a couple of months the Holy Spirit convicted him to get rid of the rifle altogether. The Lord was his shield and protection. "That first night without it," he laughs, "I was sorely tested by the devil."

As he lay in bed reading the Bible strange noises came from the verandah. His imagination began to run riot, "They've cut through the fence, they're surrounding the house, they've cut the telephone wires, it's Kufa Ufulu coming at last, they're going to burst into the door any minute." As Jonathan imagined each horror his heart was pounding faster and faster. Suddenly he realized the trap and with a loud voice declared, "so what if they kill me, I'll be with the Lord." With that he laughed and laughed at the devil whose power was broken and Jonathan never had a problem in that area again. To prove his point, he boldly leapt out of bed, turned on all the lights in the house and marched outside to investigate. It was an owl!! He was confident that if ever stopped by terrs, God would undertake and deliver him out of the situation. But, on the other hand, if the terrs found a weapon, he was convinced there would be no help because he was relying on the "arm of flesh." He felt the same way about traveling with the convoy. It was never made a mandatory thing by the government but very few people ever traveled alone. Jonathan was one of those few, to the fury of many.

"It was very personal," explained Jonathan. "God was extending me and I never tried to impose my convictions on anyone else. I never denied God had given us human wisdom but God wanted me to be wholly cast upon Him and I was. In return I expected others to respect my position." Few ever did and it made relations in the ministry very difficult, but Jonathan was not prepared to move from the position he'd gained with the Lord. This was burning intercession and was preparation for greater days.

There was always the very real possibility of landmines. Most of his time was spent on dirt roads.

"That one," he says, "I overcame by reasoning that by the time I felt or heard the explosion I'd already be dead. Besides God is so Big I knew I could drive over a mine without detonating it - not deliberately of course! I've done it before and God had always protected."

Returning late one night to his isolated farmhouse, he saw the top of what looked like an ant heap placed in the middle of the road. There was a stalk of grass in it looking like a flag in a castle turret. Jonathan was not concerned about driving at night. To him there was no difference. The Lord never slept and is Master of both the Light and the Dark. "After all," declared Jonathan, "is not the earth the Lord's and the fullness thereof?" The adrenaline began to pump and Jonathan recalled some of his Intaff days.

"This is it!" whistled Jonathan expecting an ambush. Nothing happened! They were just letting me know they were around. Later, he would find out why there was never an attack.

One evening as he "low flew" down a very long hill he realized too late that the bend at the bottom of the hill took an almost 80 degree angle. As the "Bellet Bullet" entered the bend he felt the car begin to roll. It was already on two wheels and certainly past the center of gravity on the roll. "Here we go," he shouted, "HELP Lord!" At that immediate instant the car came to an abrupt halt and was securely back on four wheels. "I know it was an angel," he declares, "I really kept them busy and guess I almost wore out my own guardian angel."

The original settler road between Umtali and Salisbury passed through some beautiful hill country. There was a mountain pass on this dirt road. It was very treacherous. The settlers had named it "Devil's Pass" because many an ox - wagon had met its demise there. Jonathan had only ever driven up it. He loathed the name and told the devil, "you won't get me here." Well, he certainly tried. The farmers along that road like in so many districts were very isolated. Once a week Jonathan would spend a night at each farm in succession. The farmers loved the company and wanted to know what made this "Reverend" tick. It was getting dark again and Jonathan was late. He was humming along and didn't know that the Roads Department had recently cut a drainage ditch clear across the road at the top of Devil's Pass. He hit the ditch and took off about ten feet into the air. The problem was that the road fell away at a very steep angle into the pass. There was the Bellet flying through the air at almost right angles to the slope. "I'm going home, Hallelujah," he shouted. The car hit the pass and careered from cliff face side to precipice side, zigzagging down the pass. Jonathan released the steering, "Over to You Lord, I'm out!" The car was not in his control anymore. She bounced down the mountain pass like a rubber ball until she landed on a large boulder. The momentum of the vehicle dislodged the bolder and car and boulder continued bouncing down the mountain together. The car... and boulder came to a grinding halt when the boulder jammed in a water culvert about half way down. The car rocked to-and-fro like a "see saw" on the edge of the cliff. Jonathan gingerly climbed out having sustained no injuries and walked to the nearest farm to get help. The farmer was amazed. "In this terr infested place you walked? We'd better go fetch your car. There'll be nothing left of it by morning. They'll burn it." Immediately they left under armed escort to rescue the "Bellet Bullet" which had lost only the exhaust. It was a miraculous escape yet again: the mighty overshadowing wings of God had kept His servant.

Week after week, as Jonathan traveled to the farms talking, sharing, revealing the love of Jesus, each family would patiently listen and ask appropriate questions, more out of politeness than conviction. Nobody seemed to make a decision for the Lord. "At times I was tempted to become discouraged," he confessed, "but that would have been taking the responsibility of the ministry into my own hands when it was clearly God's. I knew that I was fully cast upon Him and walking through that death process of which He had spoken. For any instrument to be effective for God in His way and on His terms, there must be a death to everything that is self. This is the cross experience and so necessary for every believer. Without the cross there will be a work and even results but it will never truly be His and there will never flow from the vessel pure streams of living water. That is what the Holy Spirit is desiring in our lives: a well of Living Water; Zoe life which continually fills the temple of our bodies and flows out to touch the world and supply the real needs of a lost and dying humanity."

The natives in the farm compounds would eagerly listen to the Word and the farmers were more than co-operative in allowing Jonathan the liberty to preach to them. Being tobacco-growing areas, the farms were labor intensive. The smallest farms would employ as many as three hundred workers. They "ranched" tobacco rather than grew it. During curing season, hundreds of barns dotted everywhere, would belch forth smoke, "but", says Jonathan, "I must confess the smell of cured tobacco was pleasant. I would often resort to one of the barns for a quick sauna amongst the curing tobacco where the heat would soar to 180 degrees and humidity was often 100 percent. It was more a steam bath than sauna."

It was these laborers who were open to the Gospel. They listened intently and flocked forward when it came to making a decision. But then, the same people flocked forward every night as they do in Africa. Some people ended up giving their lives to the Lord thirty times or more! "I just wondered how saved they felt they had to get," recalls Jonathan "and no matter how much you explained, they still came forward. Usually they were the ones who were not saved. The only real indication as with everyone, was not responding to an appeal but seeing changed lives. And, many lives did change. I always aimed for the `big fish' in any compound. When he came in the others followed. That was rewarding but I knew things would really change if the farmers and their wives surrendered."

A year after he left the area a mini revival did take place in that farming community and over one hundred and twenty started attending church. Lives were changed and people were set on fire for Jesus. It turned the whole district and had long-lasting effects. "One sows and another reaps but it is God who gives the increase." How Jonathan rejoiced at that increase. The unseen hand of the Almighty was slowly fashioning His sharp threshing tool for the future. God was opening the native work to Jonathan and gently leading him down that avenue. How his heart burned for them. They too loved his preaching, loved his being with them. He was always laughing and joking, always playing with the children and interested in their lives and they responded. This was true missionary work in the sea of lost humanity with all its heartaches, problems and complexities.

It was while engaged in such work that Jonathan met with Felix again. He had become a security guard at a paper factory situated in the vast pine forests of Inyanga. Felix was overjoyed to see Jonathan. He shared how he'd run away because he hated the life of "Mr. Tony" and at the time feared he might not be strong enough to stand. But stood he had, and without any training or even knowing the Bible, he'd started a church and had about forty factory workers attending regularly. Together, he and Jonathan worked and built the church into a strong base and soon had teams traveling and evangelizing. Felix was later ordained and moved to Chipinga with Jonathan where they worked together in mission outreach. He became a faithful and devoted servant to both the Lord and Jonathan. Oh the faithfulness of God to take an ordinary person and transform him into a mighty warrior is beyond our comprehension. God's ways are not our ways and He does indeed take the weak things to confound the wise and the lowly to humble the lofty. This was Felix. What hope there is in God's mighty power. He's taken a simple village boy on his deathbed, turned his life around, equipped him for service and launched him into a dynamic ministry. Felix would cycle, walk or bus hundreds of miles every month to preach the Gospel in some most remote areas. He would establish Bible study groups and lead them into maturity to become fully-fledged churches. What zeal, what commitment, what sacrifice to fulfill the high calling of God with such little resources. Men who abide faithful under such circumstances - and Felix was one - are destined to be great in God's eyes. Felix is a great man.

The "Bellet Bullet" traveled thousands of miles, whistling down the mountain passes, up to the tea estates along the Mocambique border, into the plantations and to the most remote, isolated farms. Jonathan remembers vividly a very humorous incident one night but also very embarrassing. The Inyazura district was strongly Dutch Reformed Calvinists and certainly not open to the Gospel, especially "tongue talking" and water baptism by immersion. Jonathan had targeted a young "elite" couple who, in his estimation were the "Big Fish." Young married couples ran most of the farms in the area and this couple was like the local "trend setters." Danie's father owned seventeen tobacco "ranches" and his mother had several of her own. They were very well to do and had a magnificent home. Jonathan befriended them and through that avenue, lived Jesus before them. Hanli was an accomplished singer and he was always encouraging her to sing for the Lord. Most happily today, she is South Africa's top Gospel singer composing many of her own songs. When Danie felt Jesus begin to convict he said, "I don't want Jonathan in this house anymore. You tell him Hanli!" Hanli had become gloriously filled with the Holy Ghost one night. Her greatest desire then was to be Baptized in water. This was an enormous step for a "leading light" in a very traditional community. She told Jonathan what her precious husband had said and he simply laughed and continued his visiting. They were a tremendous support and encouragement to Jonathan and they loved to debate but not to vainless disputation. Danie eventually became gloriously saved after their move to South Africa in 1980.

Well, it was one night when Jonathan was visiting that they had finished dinner and were sitting sharing. Suddenly there was an "explosion" somewhat muffled but clearly an "explosion" followed by two more in rapid succession. "We all looked at each other aghast. This was it! With all my experience," said Jonathan, "it was unmistakable." The lights were hurriedly distinguished and Hanli rushed to the bedrooms to drag the kids from their beds and take them into the safe area. Two more bombs "exploded" but strangely there was no AK47 rifle fire. Danie hit the Agric-Alert button to notify the police that the farm was under attack. He threw Jonathan a rifle and both of them slid out of the window and took off towards the fence. It was strangely quiet. They crawled along listening, waiting. Absolutely nothing. In the distance they heard the Police Reserve approaching. And then, to their horror and dismay, the unbelievable: the horse kicked the stable door again. It sounded just like a mortar exploding. Two very embarrassed and red-faced men had some explaining to do.... The Police were not amused!!

The eastern part of Rhodesia was a stronghold of satan because homes of renowned 'nangas (witchdoctors) were situated in strategic places throughout the province. Through strong intercessions the Holy Spirit directed Jonathan to attack such strongholds. That battle raged for several years. There was one particular place that was most significant and lay within the realms of his "parish." The highest peak in Rhodesia was Mt. Inyangani. It was an ominous place. The local natives spoke of "human sacrifice" on the mountain and that strong witches "lived up there." It was a known fact that strange mists would descend on the mountain causing hikers to become lost and disappear. The last case was a party of children who were on a school hike. In broad daylight on a clear day the mist descended. A straggling boy was lost and he was never found despite a massive hunt which included using the best trackers available and helicopters to search in places where man could not go. One day the Holy Spirit commanded Jonathan, "Redeem that Mountain." With selected friends who understood the ways of the Spirit they climbed the most aggressive face of Inyangani. They began early in the morning just as daylight was cracking the eastern sky. It was quite a trail and they reached the summit at about midday after stopping to pray at various spots. It was a clear, beautiful, sunny day. There was not a cloud in the sky as far as the eye could see.

"It was incredible," reported Jonathan some years later. "We sat down to celebrate the Lord's Supper after which we were 'directed' to cast the remaining emblems on the mountain and claim it for Jesus. No sooner had we sat down to begin communion than a strong wind started blowing. It soon was quite violent and without warning a mist did, in fact, begin to appear. We knew that it was the powers of darkness. As pharaoh's magicians had performed diabolic miracles before Moses, I had no doubt that the 'nangas were doing the same thing before us. It was eerie. As the mist swirled around we partook of the emblems and then began to cast the rest of the bread and 'wine' to the wind with powerful prayers. As we poured out the 'wine' we bound up the enemy and put the whole mountain and its activities 'under the power of the Blood of Jesus.' Immediately, the wind stopped and the mist, which had become thick, swirling clouds, disappeared. The day was as clear as it had been before. Some weeks later as I was traveling and visiting in the area again, a farmer who knew nothing of our little expedition remarked, 'you know, Jonathan, Mt. Inyangani has changed. It doesn't look so aggressive and menacing anymore but has taken on a softer appearance.'" There was never another disappearance on the mountain nor even a reported case of the eerie mist again. The powers of darkness were broken. Jesus had brought the victory and strong powers of witchcraft were broken enabling many areas to be open to the Gospel.

Many in the area had a problem with the way in which Jonathan traveled during those dangerous and difficult war years but he was not foolish in his travels and depended on the guidance of the Holy Spirit. Sometimes he had the clear direction not to proceed and he would always obey. "It happened one night," he said, "that my fuel tank started to empty at an alarming rate." Fuel was not purchasable after 6.00 p.m. "I had traveled the route many times and knew just how much fuel I needed to get home. But, there I was, only half way and my tank was nearly empty. I had watched the gauge and seen its descent. There was an hotel along the route which sold petrol (gas) and I was 'compelled' to stay the night and put in fuel the next morning. Only God knew the many unseen dangers that lurked in the bush. At other times He revealed some of the secrets not only to show His awesome power but also to show me just how much He loved me. God is so personal and it is that personal touch which makes Him so endearing. What a God we serve."

About a hundred and twenty miles south of Umtali, there was another large farming community in the very hot, humid, low-lying Sabi Valley, home of the crocodiles. Part of the valley was one huge irrigated basin stretching about forty miles long and eight miles wide. The farmers grew wheat in winter and soya beans in summer. Most of the affluent farmers lived in Salisbury and left their farms under the direction of managers. A strong work had been established in the valley as a branch of the Umtali Assemblies of God. This was not Jonathan's area but he was often asked to fill in for his colleagues. It just so happened one long weekend that there was to be a series of meetings and Jonathan was asked to take them. Due to some complications, he was very late leaving and started praying that the Lord would get him there on time. It was, even for the "Bellet Bullet," an impossibility. The main tar road passed along the edge of his old stomping ground, Maranke Tribal Trust Land. As he "low flew" Jonathan thought about Ufulu. He hadn't thought of him in quite a while. About thirty miles out of Umtali as it was getting dusk, an incredible fear descended on Jonathan.
"What is it Lord, is there an ambush? Must I turn back?" as he slowed the car. The clear unmistakable voice of the Lord came back,
"No, proceed you'll be all right. I am with you."
With that, Jonathan pressed the accelerator to the floor and the Bellet took off again. What Jonathan didn't immediately realize was that the Bellet had in fact literally taken off. Jonathan recalls, "I shook my head in amazement because I was inexplicably and immediately at the junction to Middle Sabi. I suddenly realized that I had not been conscious of passing very familiar landmarks on the road I knew so well. I looked at my watch. It was impossible: less than two minutes seemed to have gone by since asking the Lord if I should proceed. Here I was about ten miles from my destination. I concluded I must have dozed or dreamed as I drove and that my watch had stopped. I knew I should be at least an hour forty-five minutes late for the meeting. I was convinced something had gone terribly wrong but all the gauges on the vehicle were in perfect working order and my watch just continued ticking the seconds."
Arriving at the house he was confused. There were no cars. He rushed in to be met by his host who assured him that he had arrived in good time.

"Impossible!" blurted Jonathan, "I know I'm horribly late."
"But how did you come?" asked his host. "There was a major concentration of terrs this morning on the road. They had to call in the choppers (helicopters) to escort the convoy and those gooks (another colloquial term for terrs) are still around!" There have been attacks all day. How did you get here? You amaze me, Jonathan."
It was then that Jonathan realized... realized that he had been going into an ambush and not only had the car been lifted over the danger areas but it had been transported some eighty miles down the road all in less than a minute. Well, it had happened to the disciples in Galilee and to Phillip who was "caught away" from the Ethiopian Eunuch in Acts and certainly they were living in the Church Age or the Acts of the Holy Spirit. Our God IS the same yesterday, today and forever. "How the Spirit descended on the meeting that night as we celebrated. We were caught up into His presence and continued in the power for almost four hours," Jonathan clearly remembers. What a victory! Once again, the devil had been defeated and the Lord had shown His mighty hand on the behalf of those who love Him. All the Lord requires is a yielded vessel, and, after all, his servant had become "recklessly abandoned" for the Lord. "It can happen to anyone," explained Jonathan. "All we have to do is be out there in that zone where the Spirit will move that way."
As Jonathan's year at Inyazura drew to an end, so did the long terrorist war. International overseers were in the country to prepare and monitor "free and fair" elections. The terrorists were supposed to gather in certain designated "assembly points" where they would be housed in big tent villages. A large group gathered outside the homestead of one of the neighboring farmers. There was a great deal of suspicion and trepidation but after sometime, the farmer engaged them in conversation, asking them where they had been based, how long they'd been in the area and many other related questions. Eventually, one of the terr leaders pointed in the direction of where Jonathan lived and asked what went on at that house "because we very afraid of that place." The farmer laughed,
"But I thought you weren't supposed to be afraid of anything. Why should you be afraid of that farm? Only a wild young preacher man lives there."
"No, no!" they all chorused. "You are cheating us. We seen an army of very big, big shiny soldiers every night and we too afraid

to go near. Everyone walk far around that place. Ugh no, we no like that place.... We wanted many times to attack and ambush there but we too afraid...."

The New Year of 1980 was actually the start of a decade of new beginnings in the life and ministry of Jonathan. Little did he know what lay ahead of him. If God should reveal all in advance we never would be able to contain it. He is so gracious in His dealings with His people to patiently walk step by step with them until they conquer each hurdle in their progress to a higher level with the Lord. God always purposes that his people make progress in their walk with Him. That is what real prosperity is: advancing and going up to a higher plane with the Holy Spirit. Most of God's people are too happy and content to stay or to abide where they are. That's why God can seldom move mightily on behalf of His people. Some walk, some trot while others run.

And thus closed a vast chapter in the life of Jonathan. God had brought him through and was about to burst on the shores of His servant's life in a new and dynamic way. Certainly there had been a death sentence upon him in more ways than one. Physically he was still alive but there was much more still to come. Would he continue to live?

CHAPTER EIGHT

REVIVAL

Chipinge, nestled in the beautiful rolling hills of South East Zimbabwe, is also a traditional Dutch Reformed community. It is in these rolling hills that the majority of the nation's coffee farms and tea plantations are situated. It is also a prominent dairy-farming district. The whole community was heavily hit during the war years: ambushes, homestead attacks, landmines. But, the people have always been tough and resilient and continue to be so. They refused to be intimidated, they refused to be driven off the land and refused to yield their heritage. Everyone is an aunt, uncle, cousin, nephew, niece, brother or sister; called in Afrikaans, "Die Familie." Win the patriarch of the clan and you will them all; offend though and you alienate all.

It was into this area - in fact forty miles north of Chipinge - that true Holy Ghost revival came in 1906 under God's servant and intercessor, Rees Howells. As intercession with its accompanying life of prayers and fastings had gripped Jonathan, he had naturally become acquainted with Rees Howell's "Intercessor," and description of how the Holy Ghost fell through the travail of His servant. Rusitu was devastated by the terrorists during the war and seemed a hard place. The Spirit however clearly spoke that the devil hated the places of great revival. The Holy Spirit shared that He was more than willing to come down again even in that very spot because places where He had fallen were and always remained special to Him. "They are hallowed grounds," said the Spirit. "I will not yield an inch of territory to the enemy." At the same time, the devil knowing this does all in his power by corrupting the natural things to prevent the Holy Ghost moving again. The powers of darkness do this by making places hard with sin, difficult to live or simply unappealing to the natural senses. That is why a person cannot and must not be led by their natural senses. "I need a yielded vessel through which I can flow," the

Spirit spoke to Jonathan, "a band of dedicated men and women who will give their all for me just as the early apostles did."

A long fast ensued during which Jonathan stayed in a tent by a river. The Holy Ghost spoke again, "Ask of Me and I will give the Nations as an inheritance for you and the ends of the earth for your possession." Could it possibly be true that God would indeed give the nations? And so, beginning with Genesis, Jonathan mapped through God's Word, just how much God loves and is concerned for the nations; that He has a redemptive plan for the nations and is today still looking for that great sea of peoples from every nation, kindred, tribe and tongue to come before Him and worship Him.

One of the first Bible studies that followed was looking at the covenant God had made with Abraham. It was awesome how that same covenantal God descended in the midst of the group and challenged each one to make a covenantal commitment to Him. "We all knew that we were under the Blood of Jesus but this was something very different. That incredible, almost tangible, presence of God was in the place. We were so forcibly struck by the Lord's command to Abraham to look at the stars that we felt exercised in the same way. Enlargement of the soul takes place; one no longer looks on the human frailties and impossibilities but on the vastness of a limitless Father. We left the room and gathered in a large circle under the canopy of a magnificent African night. The air was cool, even a little crisp. Looking to the stars we were silent for some considerable time. We could feel our hearts enlarging as we realized only God could do this handiwork and if He did all this, what more could He do with us? It was settled right there and then. Nobody was forced but those who covenanted with God that night to be His vessels, were set aside. The Spirit came upon us; we were drenched in Him, immersed, and overwhelmed so much so that we thought we were going to be snatched away. Heaven had again come down to touch mortal man. We became "other men." That same Bible Study was held in three different places during the next week and the anointing fell each time. God was molding a team who would be "recklessly abandoned" to Him. Oh, the unfathomable riches of an incredible God are beyond our wildest imaginations. How God's people have restrained Him through their unbelief."

About ten miles south of Middle Sabi, which came directly under Jonathan's ministry was a large assembly point. This is where terrorists had been required to gather for the cease-fire. Though they were supposed to remain in their camps these terrs marauded and terrorized the local populace. Anybody who did not co-operate with them was fed to the crocodiles infesting the Sabi River. Half eaten bodies were often dragged from the river and large numbers of crocodiles had gathered in particular spots expecting to receive their human morsels. It was into this camp, "Tongogara", that Jonathan ventured to preach. The hostility towards an intruder, especially a hated white man was quite terrifying in the natural. "Without the power of God's presence and His peace, I would have been demolished," Jonathan had declared. "I walked into this camp of several thousand men and it was like entering the frigid zones of the Arctic. Hostility was in the air; those man bristled with hate and anger and frustration not least because they had been promised they would have everything - farms, cars, houses - for the taking yet there they were, seven months later still cooped up in the midst of the harsh Sabi Lowveld.

They were not going to welcome this white man in his "Bellet-Bullet." "It was one of the hardest assignments I ever had from the Holy Spirit: arriving in the camp with the greatest gift to man: the love of Jesus and then to be rejected before even starting was very difficult. That first evening I arrived, about two thousand men were running for physical exercise. It was hot and sticky but more so for me because once in the midst of the men, I realized they could turn over the vehicle and smash it to pieces with me inside. That is exactly how they felt: frustrated and ready to take it out on anyone. It just so happened that I was "the anyone". Yes, I was very nervous in the natural but there was that unseen presence of God giving power and a deep peace within. It is that kind of energizing strength that makes you want to rise up and conquer the world for Jesus."

Jonathan headed directly for the camp commanders. He was ushered into the presence of four young men about his own age. They too were hostile and aggressive. One thing that will win one over very quickly with natives is the ability to laugh at oneself. They spoke perfect English and were not uneducated men. Jonathan quickly set to work at putting them at ease and what a job it was. He wondered if he would end up as crocodile meat and knew that one order from these commanders and he would be a prisoner whom nobody, not even the new communist government could rescue. The camps were a world of their own and the commanders a law unto themselves. They had the power of life and death. They could arrest and have a man flogged simply because they did not like the look of his face. Minor misdemeanors among the men were punishable by being locked in a sweatbox for days; no water, no movement and little air in the midst of the heat which reached 120 degrees in the shade and humidity often hovering in the 90's.

"God alone was my refuge and strength. Without Him, I was done for," laughed Jonathan later. "It was a world of iniquity in that camp. There were no restraints and the local people - especially women and young maidens - suffered most. Pregnancies and sexual diseases were rife and there was little or no treatment. There was nothing for the men to do all day but get drunk on local brew, gamble and womanize: fertile breeding ground for pure wickedness and lawlessness. Commander Jumo was in charge. Once the ice was broken with him, the remaining three mellowed." They were soon laughing at Jonathan and teasing him. He laughed at himself with them and was pressed to stay for the evening meal. "To have refused would have been an insult and offended them. They were delighted that I would partake of their sadza and relish or gravy. It is unappetizing food but without it the natives feel as though they are dying. The sadza consisted of stiff boiled corn meal which is rolled into balls with the fingers and dipped into the relish. That evening they were sharing their best, their delicacy. That `delicacy' was the unclean tripe - the stomach that looks like a dirty green towel - of an ox cut into pieces around which is twined lengths of the intestine. The lumps of offal are slightly fried and then boiled until `tender.' It becomes a greenish color, smells nauseating and is worse to eat." Jonathan wanted to pass dinner but didn't and made sure that he swallowed without chewing and that the relish did not stick in his throat. As the balls of sadza and lumps of intestine passed down, Jonathan felt like an ostrich looks with an orange slipping down its long scrawny neck. Juma was delighted as they ate and soon the subject switched on to Marxist Dialectic. To the men's utter amazement Jonathan began to demolish their arguments using all the appropriate jargon. Slowly and skillfully he maneuvered the conversation to the Gospel. This time it was his surprise. Juma and his friends knew all about religion: they had plenty of academic knowledge about Jesus and the Kingdom of God without having a personal knowledge of Him. The four had been to mission schools; one even to seminary but it had made no difference in their lives. These men had been disillusioned with life and that disillusionment had driven them to be terrorists. Now they were disillusioned with the peace which robbed them of all they believed and for which they had been fighting. The benefits they had been promised had not materialized but above all, these men had been robbed of the gift of life: cheated, deceived and lied to about who they were and what they were doing.

"And where was Garry and what was he doing at this time?" wondered Jonathan. Had that mysterious little boy obtained all his hearts desires? Time alone would tell. Time would reveal him in his true role.

The meal completed, Jonathan shared a little longer and asked if he might visit again and bring a film. He had the idea of "The Cross and the Switchblade." He knew they would love it. With one foot in the door, Jonathan aimed at having two. It was well after dark when he left and could only praise God for yet another victory. It was God and God alone Who had broken down the barriers and won over the terrorist commanders.

The film was a great success but Jonathan felt not to make any appeals. Other films followed and literature and Bibles were freely distributed but no appeals were made for the men to be committed. Vast numbers attended the films. There was nothing else for them to do. After several months of seeding the ground, Jonathan announced that there would be a full crusade from Friday through Sunday. He borrowed a large flatbed truck from one of the local farmers to act as a stage and to carry all the equipment. That truck was brand new. The crusade was held a little distance from the camp both to attract local villagers and also to bring out of the camp those who were really interested. Friday evening's two thousand or so swelled to many more on Saturday. Something was not right though: there was confusion in the air. The singing and testimonies led into the preaching. Some hecklers began to whistle and mutter and shout. Soon, there was a wave of unrest and without warning stones, sticks and bottles began flying through the air. Jonathan's interpreter rose about three feet into the air to do a "road-runner" take-off when the hand of Jonathan reached out and grabbed his collar. "Interpret," Jonathan said as he preached faster and faster. By this time the team had deserted him. All he could think about was, "Lord, what am I going to tell the owner of the truck if it's demolished? Please HELP!" Debris was lying all over the platform. It seemed though that God had put a protective shield in front of Jonathan and his interpreter: not a single projectile touched either of them. Jonathan stopped preaching. The noise of several thousand reached a crescendo. Jonathan stood his ground, raised his hands to heaven and began to pour out his heart to God. There was nothing else to do. This was a crisis! Death and destruction were at the door. It was not long - seemingly - and the noise began to subside. Jonathan dared not to open his eyes. The noise grew quieter and quieter until it stopped completely. There was a presence of God - that awesome presence as when only God comes down to His people. And what had He brought? An incredible Baptism of love! The hearts of everyone was bowed low with the love of God. The black people are a "no touch" people but there they were hugging each other and loving each other. That could be only God's doing. The violence had given way to gentleness, the anger to peace and joy. That was true brotherhood; not man's wisdom and programs but the Holy Spirit drawing all men under His umbrella. And then, the incredible was revealed. Some of the men from the camp surrounded the entire meeting. A person here and another there were escorted from the crowd. The men were standing guard to ensure continued peace and order. Those removed had been trouble-shooters and Jonathan was later told they were severely punished but not fed to crocodiles. Weeks of sowing seed were then bearing fruit. The Holy Spirit had been touching hearts all along and only He would receive the glory. There was no need for appeals, for altar calls, not even a need for preaching. God had come and everyone knew it. In His forgiving, compassionate way, He had visited the outcasts; the rejected; the sinners and left His mark upon lives that were twisted and tangled. He gave yet another chance to bitter and battered men to walk in peace and the straight path of His design. How merciful is God to give men so many opportunities to inherit the beauty, riches and glory of Jesus Christ.

It was not long after the event that Tongogara Camp ceased to be a base for those who had fought in the war. It became a center for Mocambican refugees. They were fleeing from the ravages of their war. God's timing is so perfect. The outreach work of reaching the lost, which was the burden of Jonathan's heart, had begun in earnest.

True ministry must be a natural expression of the inward workings of the Holy Spirit in a person's life. The Holy Spirit was, indeed, working in the lives of the fellowship He was establishing in Chipinge. In the midst of tradition and bondage He was visiting His Divine Apostolic order and government for the purpose of taking His Gospel to the uttermost parts of the earth. One characteristic was markedly revealed: love. There was a burning love for God which was given expression in radical praise and worship so that, with David, the people cried, "we will be yet more vile on the morrow.' There was a sacrificial love for one another, which expressed itself as 1 Cor. 13 in living action. There was a zealous love, which imparted a compassion for the lost and a desire to reach the unreached and proclaim the amazing love of God. The fellowship was ready to do anything for the Lord; to give their all materially and physically, to go to any place and to allow the Lord to work deep within. In that covenant relationship it was as if God had asked, "is anything too difficult...." and with the enlargement, which had come through the Holy Spirit, faith had to reach out and say, "Nay Lord, we believe." It all began with Him and all ended with Him. "We were just obedient vessels who wanted to please," and with such a team, God could do wonders. Not that all was rosy. There was much breaking and the continual death process was at work in everyone to bring that dependence on the Spirit alone without which so much of the work is of "self." There must come a point where there is no confidence in flesh.

The most outstanding factor of Chipinge days was that the Holy Spirit always had freedom to move. There was a fear of offending Him in the smallest way. He brought that unity and love which was a launching pad for greater things. Man's unity always brings a "Babel" but the Holy Spirit's unity always brings a "Pentecost" and Pentecost came again. One of the hallmarks of His moving on the little band in Chipinge was a burden for intercession. Most believers see intercession as some sort of intensified prayer. It is not. Intercession is a way of life; a burden planted by the Holy Spirit, nourished by Him and final victory gained through Him. Such burdens are not parochial but deal with eternal issues. So many Christians get caught up in a prayer ritual: praying for things, families and local personal situations. This has a place but is often to the exclusion of major issues which the eye of the Spirit observes and longs to deal accordingly but few intercessors are found. And so it was, that intercession with its accompanying fasting and prayers came to dominate the fellowship and create a burden for the nations.

"We came to really understand 'groanings which cannot be uttered' as we travailed and carried the burdens of the Holy Spirit. Sometimes a burden would be with us for weeks or even months extending into years before a place of intercession was gained and victory won," says Jonathan. The intercessions became a way of life and not mere meetings. The fellowship was vitally involved with the affairs of the community and there was always abundant joy. People often observe intercessors as miserable and dull, carrying such a weight. This is not so. In fact, because of the seriousness of the call there is greater joy to offset it. Jesus was a man full of fun. One of the earliest intercessions was for the British/Argentine war. The Spirit revealed that there was going to be war long before any troubles began and that He wanted the military dictatorship in Argentina overthrown. The country was to be released from military and Papish control for the Gospel to go forth in full freedom. The fellowship went into action and the Holy Spirit began to reveal the burdens and sufferings of the Argentine peoples. None of the fellowship had ever been there but now they were taken by the Spirit into the prisons, the cities and the villages and shown the fears, miseries and bondages of a whole nation which was sighing and crying. God, indeed, was hearing and answering. Throughout the days of that short war, the fellowship was not directed by what the news media had to say but by the perceptive eye of the Holy Spirit who sees the end from the beginning. The meetings themselves - for there were daily intercessions - would move through burden and travail to victory with accompanying shouts, singing and dancing. What a time of triumph as release upon release came to the Argentine peoples. The fellowship felt the awesome responsibility that God had laid upon them in the small part He called them to play. History records the rest but never the deeper eternal issues which are involved. The eternity of a nation was at stake and that's the biggest difference between God and man. God is always vitally concerned with eternal destinies whereas man becomes embroiled in temporal affairs. There was much intercession for the communist lands in those days. The Spirit took different individuals into the prisons, the asylums, the hospitals and even the homes of the elite to experience their sufferings, trials, torments and fears. One clear revelation was that nobody was free. The demonic system of communism was an all-embracing prison for everyone but God also showed that He was also hearing the sigh and cry of the communist peoples and in particular, the blood of the multitudes of martyrs was crying out from the ground. That was encouragement enough to continue with strong intercessions for freedom to come and the whole system to break down. In true intercession one cannot depend on any natural knowledge or experience. The key must be to carry the Holy Spirit's burden as He leads into all truth and He knows what He wants to accomplish. We are merely His agents and must be obedient to His will alone.

"I well remember protracted intercession for the uprooting of witchcraft in our area. One evening the Holy Spirit took us into the Equatorial forests of Zaire," discloses Jonathan. "He revealed a vast area of the jungles under the strong control of a powerful witchdoctor and the Gospel was unable to penetrate the area despite repeated attempts. `I want him removed,' commanded the Holy Spirit and the team went to prayer. The word was that this one cometh not out but by prayer and fasting. A twenty-one day fast was proclaimed to dislodge the prince demon which ruled the Zairian jungles. It is impossible for natural changes to take place until the ruling principality has been dealt with. The devil hates fasting because like nothing else, it brings the anointing which breaks the yoke. Throughout the period of fasting, there were protracted prayers in which we were so taken into those jungles that we felt as if we were actually living there. That primitive darkness was overwhelming and how we cried for the light to penetrate. Those people desperately needed the civilization of the Gospel. They were so steeped in the darkness of their animism and the bondage of fear that there would never be an improvement in their lot. Their witchdoctors held the entire society captive and that yoke was to be broken. The last day of the fast saw a tremendous victory. "In the Spirit we saw the darkness broken and the demonic principalities come crashing. With that, the burden ended. What praises and shouts and dances of victory we enjoyed." declared Jonathan.

Many months later a member of the fellowship was en route to Europe and landed in Kinshasa. A Belgian missionary boarded the flight and sat next to him. He began to recount a most amazing story. The missionary told how he had worked in the remote parts of the Zairian jungles which he had been trying to penetrate for twenty years with the Gospel. A very strong witchdoctor and powerful forces of darkness had bound the area.

"Every year, he said, "we would visit the chief and ask for permission to preach and set up a mission. Every year we were refused. The chief was very hard and under the control of this very evil witchdoctor. His young son however, was extremely sympathetic having attended one of our schools and became converted. Suddenly a few months ago and without warning, both the witchdoctor and chief dropped dead. The son has taken over and we have free access to the whole area. A revival is taking place." The time of their death was the last day of the twenty-one day fast. The intercessions paved the way for different members of the fellowship to travel to the nations as God opened the doors. Teams traveled to Egypt, Israel, India, Europe, Uganda, Kenya and other nations, carrying the Gospel and preaching to the captives as led by the Holy Spirit.

One of the primary burdens of the fellowship was for the rural natives of their Judea and Samaria. Vast areas of rural Africa have never been properly reached with the Gospel and certainly there is a great lack of teaching throughout the Continent. Numerous places have never seen missionaries. Jonathan's greatest burden and desire was to see true revival break out in the villages and across the bush country. Much time was devoted to prayer and fasting for God's Spirit to move. Teams traveled out to different places for ministry, establishing churches and investing precious time in raising up local leadership. It was in the Rusitu valley that the Spirit first moved. "I knew that God's Spirit was waiting to move again as He had done in the days of Rees Howells," says Jonathan. "The place was bombarded with tract distribution. We dropped over 100,000 tracts across the valley from the air and sent out teams visiting individual homes and entire villages. We began to feel the extraordinary stirrings of the Holy Spirit throughout the valley." Each weekend a team would travel out from the fellowship. The road twisted through the mountains: in the dry winter the dust covered everything with a thick red powder; in summer the roads turned to slippery red clay or glassy smooth during light drizzle. No matter what the hindrances and difficulties there was no price too big to see God move. And move He did!

Camp was always pitched next to the fast flowing Rusitu River surrounded by the majestic mountains which declared the glory of God. A large open ground served for the crusade meetings. At the top of the ground was an old community hall which had neither roof nor outer walls. It was there that the stage was erected.

Winter had come and heavy dew fell in the early evening. Everything was carpeted with frost and ice as the morning mists were stirred by the sun's rays. But, despite the cold, despite the damp and despite the miles, people came. The hundreds became thousands each night as the Word of God went forth. It wasn't the miracles and healings that were sought: it was the brokenness of souls; tears of contrition, voices crying out "what must we do to be saved?" Indeed there had been much sowing in tears, travails and fastings and there was that expectancy to reap.

The word went forth with amazing power. During the meeting on the fifth night, suddenly there was a great sigh as if the entire crowd had let out one huge breath. Immediately upon it came an anguished cry followed by the sobbing of many souls. Soon, the cries and sobs were caught up by hundreds of voices so that preaching became impossible. People were being convicted and melted before the tangible presence of the Holy Spirit.

Counselors were not enough nor could ever hope to deal with the souls who were smitten by God's Holy Presence. Soon the whole field was caught up in one voluminous wail that echoed off the mountains and filled the entire valley. God was dealing with the hearts of men and His real dealings are always most deep. His presence was awesome and He was given complete liberty to do as He desired.

Each night for the next few evenings, the same phenomena occurred as God's Spirit moved among the people. There was no place for testimonies as people were breaking through to victory. The whole valley was touched and multitudes of lives eternally changed. Many were called into the work of God from that valley.

As the week drew to a close the cries and wails, the sighs and tears began to be turned into shouts of joy and victory. The last evening was a taste of heaven on earth; the supernatural tabernacling amidst the natural; the eternal with the temporal. It was an evening of praise and worship; a time of rejoicing and thanksgiving for all that God had done. As the praises ascended physically higher and higher, people began to get caught up in the air, others were slain in the Spirit and the whole multitude began to speak in other tongues.

Oh what joy it was in seeing God so supernaturally move. The Spirit flowed out of that valley and began to touch key places throughout the whole district. As the teams moved from place to place they carried revival fires with them. Whole schools and communities were transformed by the saving power of the Almighty God. It was like living in the Book of Acts all over again.

Eighty miles from Rusitu in the dry arid Sabi Valley a team was dispatched to a large secondary school. The students were very hostile and skeptical. There was no doubt that the enemy had been hard at work to bind the hearts and minds of the people and they were still living the war. Jonathan was leading the crusade in the school hall and as he was about to start, God gave a vision of the whole area being under an enormous glass-like dome of satanic control. But, praise was to be the key in that place and as the praises of the people ascended those praises began to shatter that glass and satan was seen fleeing like a dog with his tail between his legs; he'd dropped the bone!

The anointing came immediately upon a chorus "Hallelujah Amen" and the more it was sung the greater became the anointing. The natives have that timeless ability to sing repetitively for long periods. It is powerful when the anointing is on a song especially with their incredible harmony. After some two hours of the same song, the anointing was so heavy that they were compelled to cry out "enough Lord or we die." There was no hysteria or mass emotion and for the most part the students were unsaved. Like Rusitu, however, the Spirit had come. Many students had collapsed under the power of the anointing; others were staggering as drunken men while yet others were sobbing as they clutched their friends. The glass dome had completely shattered.

There was no need of preaching; there never is when God turns up in that fashion: He simply does it all. There, right in the middle of the African bush: dry, dusty, hot; no air conditioners, no electricity, no running water, God visited a secondary school and changed the lives of its students forever. The River of Life flowed out from that school to touch village upon village in the whole area. They were certainly days of heaven on earth and made one so very hungry for eternity with the King. Having tasted that reality, nothing can ever satisfy except Him and more of Him.

Yes, indeed there were the healings and miracles. There has to be when supernatural touches natural but way and above - far above - was the healing of spirit and soul. Witchdoctors and demoniacs were set free and sat at the feet of the Master in their right minds. Of course, there were those who resisted but they were always exposed.

"I well remember the biggest Baptism at which I officiated, if you can call it that!" Laughs Jonathan. "It was held in a river which flowed a mile or so from the school. There must have been over five hundred for Baptism by 7 o'clock in the morning. As the day drew on, the numbers increased and though there were eight teams baptizing, we seemed never to finish. The people kept coming. We baptized until my arms were beyond dropping off and until my legs were frozen stiff beyond feeling in the icy waters from the mountains.

It was impossible to screen every person but I found that the waters of Baptism did their own screening. One thing I had discovered was that demons hate water! I do believe it is because they well remember the pre-Adamite flood, Noah's flood and Pharaoh's drowning in the Red Sea. Every time a demoniac was put under the water there was the most violent manifestation of devils followed by an immediate deliverance. I have experienced the same thing in most third world countries. The demoniacs would hiss like snakes, scream like wounded animals, slither like slippery eels, thrash the water, beat the air; BUT the demons always came out. One woman of about thirty stood on a huge rock watching the proceedings. Without warning she lifted her arms and fell some twenty feet from the rock. She hit the water full out flat on her stomach and floated off downstream. I sent some young men racing after her and as soon as they caught hold of her she began to manifest in a most violent fashion. She was set free from many devils. We never were into counting. There was nobody to try to impress and it was all of God; His work, His power, His glory.

It was always amazing to me that just two short years before this, a war had been raging where now the peace of God reigned. Not far from the school, a close friend had been shot during that war and there we were then preaching the glorious message of hope in Christ. What an equally glorious response."

The revival fires, blown by the Wind of the Spirit, spread down the eastern border mountains into the valleys and plains. Holy Spirit - powered vessels were taking the Kingdom message from their Jerusalem to Judea and Samaria and the uttermost parts. But, Jonathan carried a burden that burned deeply in his heart: tightly closed communist Mocambique that was every bit as ruthless as East Germany. Many an afternoon he would drive out to an appropriate vantage point and gaze across the border and intercede for that nation which had been closed to the Gospel for five hundred years. Not only did he intercede but also he continued with the vital courier work which had begun in Mutare.

CHAPTER NINE

UTTERMOST

Halt!" The guard shouted. Armed soldiers leading vicious German Shepherds walked around the vehicle. Barbed wire ran for miles in every direction as far as the eye could see; gun towers with menacingly trained machine guns; skull and crossbones signs depicting mine fields and border guards pacing. This was Romania's welcome. It seemed impossible for them not to find something. The vehicle was laden with Bibles - Polish, Czech, German, Romanian and Russian - microfilm, teaching materials and supplies to give to the suffering underground church. Every name and address had been committed to memory so as not to endanger those who were already under tremendous suffering. Luggage was dragged ruthlessly from every corner of the vehicle. Jonathan's heart sank as the case containing precious records was dragged out. The catch on it was broken so that it couldn't open properly and he had packed it alone. His companion, Simon had been in town collecting a few things while Jonathan had packed and they were scheduled to catch the ferry that evening crossing to Holland for their trek across Europe and behind the Iron Curtain. Now Simon was eagerly assisting to open the case assuring the guard there was nothing in it but clothing. Jonathan felt sick and offered an urgent but very silent prayer. So many times had they prayed for God to blind seeing eyes, deafen hearing ears and cause confusion to the enemy. Not only were there records in that case but precious machine parts for a vitally needed printing press. The Russian believers were anxiously awaiting those parts that would be smuggled on from Romania. That was the main purpose of the Romanian Rendezvous. Fifteen different parts were stowed in various places and each was vital to the urgent programming of the press for printing Bibles. It seemed Simon would never stop pulling back the flaps of the wretched case. And then, Oh no! The guard had plunged his hand into the case and was feeling around. It was impossible for him not to locate the records. The machine parts were small and well stowed but the records... Jonathan felt sick to his stomach... it had to be over before they had even started. Suddenly without a word he moved on to the next case. Jonathan quietly breathed a sigh of relief.

The whole land was under a choking oppression. Soviet tanks were everywhere; the Red Star in every village and city square. Nobody smiled, nobody was friendly and like all the citizens Jonathan himself kept looking over his shoulder to see who was following. So this was the "freedom" which communism had to offer? This is what little Garry had fled to Botswana to obtain. Jonathan had been given six days only on his visa pass and there was need to move quickly. The roads were in a terrible state and a soft drizzle made the bleak country even bleaker. Even the trees and animals seemed drooped under the oppression. How Jonathan longed to stop the vehicle, leap out and dance and shout and praise the Lord to break the tension. He remembered the revival meetings in Africa but this was a far cry from the African bush and impossible to be demonstrative in such bondage.

In every town there were lines for everything: meat, milk, bread, and fuel. Jonathan rejoiced that they had adequate provisions with them. At a few places they stopped for basic requirements which they had to purchase with tourist coupons. Surly attendants who seemed to object to the foreigners with their British number plates and money buying their supplies, greeted them.

Bucharest was reached on the afternoon of the second day. A cold, dull, dirty city that appeared most unwelcoming. Police and army were everywhere. Jonathan correctly concluded that if this was what was visible, how much was invisible? How many secret police and informers were lurking behind the scene? Though they had a good - sized tent they were by no means motivated to erect it in the rain with the possibility of exposing their "treasures." After several hours search they managed to find a camping ground with some primitive chalets. The paint was peeling off the walls, there was wood rot in the floors and a damp musty smell spoke spiritually of the condition of the entire land.

Throughout Eastern Europe nobody wore colorful clothes, nobody smiled and nobody was obliging. It took a whole day for Jonathan to find the home of their contact. It was necessary to park the car several blocks away and walk in another direction to ensure they were not being followed. When all was safe they made their way swiftly to the address. Two knocks only and wait. As soon as the door opened the code word must be presented immediately,

"Rahab's Ribbon." Jonathan and Simon were virtually dragged into the house and left standing while a plumpish lady with rounded face bustled off. Soon an older, bald-headed man appeared. With a warm smile and warmer embrace he introduced himself as Petre Croija and led the way into a prayer meeting. It was the first time in Romania that Jonathan had seen anyone smile. The room was filled with mainly older people who quietly rejoiced and wept as Jonathan and Simon shared about Africa and God's moving there. Jonathan had to preach in a whisper so as not to be heard through the thin walls. The group sang a hymn but ever so quietly. Jonathan's heart ached as he thought of the freedom in Africa. "Peace I leave with you, My peace give I unto you." Jesus was certainly reigning in the room and had brought His peace. What a welcome relief.

Reluctantly, individuals began to leave at intervals. It took almost an hour before the last person had left. "There is a need for caution," Petre indicated, "You can understand that meetings take a great deal of time and effort to organize but they're worth it."

Though Jonathan did not know it at the time, the Eastern European tour was not an adventure but God's testing ground for what was to come in Africa. The Holy Spirit can only use vessels that have been tried and tested in many furnaces of affliction. "I'd seen danger, been in wars, experienced the mighty hand of God's deliverance but this was different," says Jonathan. "It was a war of the nerves to which I don't think anyone could ever grow accustomed. My heart certainly reached out to those who lived there. One old lady begged us to visit her the next day. Petre agreed it would be okay. She gave us the street where to meet her and informed us that we were to follow her half a block behind. When she turned into the apartment we were to walk on past and continue round the block and then enter the building going directly to her flat on the fourth floor and enter - no knocking. If anyone was around we were to continue climbing the stairs. What a performance just to have some fellowship. I asked the lady, 'Tell me, you were obviously under the Nazi occupation of World War II. How does this compare?'

Illyana never hesitated in her reply, 'Much worse my son, much worse. Especially as we've cried for help from the West and it never came and it never comes.'

'No Sister Illyana, God Himself will deliver you as He did Israel from Pharaoh.'"

With the machine parts, the Russian and Romanian Bibles safely deposited with Petre, Jonathan and Simon turned northwest to reach Czechoslovakia. It was European summer though the men had not seen much sun. They were to hold some meetings in remote farming areas including a youth camp in the mountains of southeast Czechoslovakia. But, the Bibles and materials were to be delivered in Prague. It was very mystifying how in one area there seemed to be freedom while in another there was none. Jonathan recalled while working for Richard Wurmbrand how the moderator of the British Baptist Association had gone to Moscow and on his return had said there was religious freedom in the Soviet Union, while there were published lists of hundreds in prisons and asylums as well as authored testimonies. It was a very clever communist tactic: a house divided against itself cannot stand and here they were setting the church at loggerheads with itself.

There were incredibly moving stories of professors and scientist who had become street sweepers and suffered because of their stand for Jesus. Similarly, there were Pastors who informed on their congregations because their belly was their god. Jonathan recalled how Jesus said in Matthew, "Many shall be offended and shall betray one another and shall hate one another... and because iniquity shall abound, the love of many shall wax cold."

In such a society, there was no place for lukewarmness: either way one was hot or cold. The amazing thing was that there was no love among the communists themselves. The inter-border search was just as rigorous as at the crossing into Rumania. Jonathan asked one guard, "For what are you searching?" He gruffly replied, "Drugs, Bibles, pornography...." How ironic thought Jonathan, that the treasures of God's Word - the light unto the world - should be lumped together with the darkness of the world. The Bibles were securely rolled up in the tent, stowed under the seat and placed in the panels of the vehicle. It was plain that there was no love between Romanian and Czechs even though they rigorously followed the same ideology. They were divided through suspicion and hatred - that's exactly how the devil separates God's people. It was amazing to Jonathan that God had brought him to the lands that had supported the terrorists in the African war and trained Kufu Ufulu. Jonathan often wondered what had become of him and when he remembered, asked the Lord "Get him Lord, get him!"

The mountains of southeastern Czechoslovakia were most magnificent, dotted with their farming communities. Out in the country one could relax for the first time - a little anyway, though one always had to be on guard especially with the prized cargo that was being ferried. Jonathan and Simon were pleasantly surprised and refreshed by the meetings though there was something decidedly lacking. Jonathan couldn't quite put his finger on the problem. There were over two hundred youngsters from all parts of the country: they were warm and hospitable; appeared hungry and attentive as the Bible smugglers shared about Africa and from the Word, but something was missing. Jonathan had learned to wait for the Lord to reveal and so He did. About the fourth day a very pleasant young man in his late teens came and spoke to the men. Immediately there was that witness of the burning of the Lord in Jonathan's heart. Taking a walk along a disused goat - path Wicktor began to share his heart. "You see," he said, "we are a state registered Christian youth organization. These camps are wonderful but I'm desperately hungry for God. As you can see, most of us even have Bibles..."

"I wondered at that," said Simon.

"Well, it's because they're issued to us - it's window dressing but all this fun and everything else prevents us from really doing something for the Lord. I mean we can't evangelize on the streets or hold crusades or travel outside."

"So that's it. That's why there's no power in your meetings," said Jonathan, "and why your meetings are always cut short."

"Yes, there are always observers from the Bureaus of Religion and State Security...they monitor every meeting.... I'm sure some of them have talked to you already even although you didn't know."

"For all we know, you could be one, Wicktor," added Jonathan, "except for the witness of the Spirit."

"Indeed yes," replied the young man, "except I'm so in love with Jesus. Can't you help me? You've got something more."

"But we're leaving tomorrow for Prague, Wicktor. We'll only be there a few days and then on to Poland."

"My home is on the outskirts of Prague. You could stay with us - it's only mama, my sister and me. Papa was taken last year for Baptizing...."

"Then your house will be under observation... We'll discuss it between ourselves Wicktor and come up with something."

Jonathan and Simon faced a real dilemma. Wicktor appeared so genuine and there was the witness of the Spirit but there were several issues at stake. He could be a decoy working for the bureau in which case he was to be avoided: he could be genuine in which case it would be a tragedy
to miss an opportunity to help....
"But it's outside our mandate Simon."
"And if this is the leading of the Holy Spirit?"
"We cannot risk it. I'm all in favor of going the extra mile, of experiencing hardships and dangers but to risk all those who are relying on us.... Besides, we still have to deliver that vital microfilm in Prague. It's just too risky..."
"You're too cautious. Look how hungry this young man is."
"Yes, and look how Joshua was deceived by the Gibeonites and how the prophet was disobedient and eaten by the lion."
It was decided to spend the following day with Wicktor encouraging him and sharing with him at the home of their host and hostess a couple of miles from the camp. BUT, Wicktor did not show up.... That solved their problem.
Prague was as dirty, dull and drab as Bucharest. Huge chimneystacks belched black soot across the city and everything was covered in a fine carbon dust. It was claustrophobic. It took the whole afternoon to find their contact after settling into their camping ground. They decided to make the drop early the following evening. It was growing dark and they had at least an hours drive back to the camp. There appeared to be a lot of police about and neither Jonathan nor Simon relished the thought of being stopped. They had been warned how unscrupulous the police were and how notorious for always troubling visitors and wanting bribes. They were making good progress and well within the speed limit when Simon, who was driving, suddenly declared, "There's a blue light flashing behind us."
"Oh no! Pull over but whatever you do don't switch off the engine Simon. Just pretend you don't understand" ordered Jonathan. The policeman strutted up to the car.
"Papers," he demanded. Simon handed him his driving licenses.
"Yes! Yes! Yes! But papers?"
The most incredible thing was that the passports had been left at the camp. What a thing to happen in a communist country. Jonathan tried to explain that one could stay while the other went to fetch the papers.

"No. Leave the car and walk." demanded the policeman.
"That's impossible. It's a great distance...." declared Jonathan.
"Switch off engine..." ordered the policeman. Jonathan leaned over and whispered to Simon, "Don't - once we do that we're lost....Pretend you don't understand. His English is very poor."
"Well what exactly is the problem? Why have you stopped us?" inquired Jonathan.
"Speed. This is 60 kilometer zone."
"But we were only going 40!" said Simon.
What was the point of arguing? We were in his trap and he knew it. Jonathan could only quietly pray that he did not want to search: anything could happen then....
"Just pay, just pay," exclaimed the policeman impatiently, "one hundred Kronis." That wasn't much - about $10 - but it was the principle... Simon handed him a 100 Kronin bill. He smiled and was about to put the money in his pocket when Jonathan demanded a paper, "A receipt, please." The smile left his face and he knew that he was now trapped as he had already taken the money. Nobody was going to win the round. To save face the policeman was forced to write an official receipt and release the vehicle.
"Phew, that was close," sighed Simon and Jonathan together. As the police car overtook them they waved to show no hard feelings but the policeman was not so happy.
Solidarity had already begun to liberate Poland which was much freer than either Romania or Czechoslovakia. Two outstanding experiences took place in Poland. The first was a memorable trip to Auschwitz. The Soviets had gone to tremendous lengths to expose the Nazi atrocities in Poland but the irony was that their slave labor camps, extermination camps, prisons and asylums were equally as bad. The horrors of Auschwitz cannot adequately be described: there were the gas chambers with the cement walls clawed by countless thousands of hands in an effort to escape. The walls had had to be replastered regularly during those terrible years of the Nazi extermination. What a saga of inhumanity, indignity and suffering. How the devil has sought to wipe out God's people: true Christians and Jews. That was the very reason Jonathan and Simon were there: to bring love, hope and encouragement to those who had been labeled number one enemy of the communists: the Church of Jesus Christ and the Jews.
The sanitarium was most graphic and horrendous. It was there that experiments on the human anatomy were performed amidst

unimaginable human suffering and indignity by the famous Dr. Mengele in his main attempt to isolate cells and create the classical blonde hair and blue-eyed Nazi Arian clone for future generations. The gallows were still intact where numerous prisoners were publicly hanged and the death wall still stood where thousands were executed by firing squad, the bullets still lodged in the wall. Acres and acres are devoted to a huge museum on the exact spot depicting life exactly as it was in the extermination camps of the Holocaust. Mountains of personal belongings - spectacles, combs, shoes, brushes, suitcases, stand behind huge glass walls as mementos of the robbery and suffering inflicted on individuals.

Wherever Jonathan walked he kept smelling a strange musty acrid smell and heard a whining noise. Every now and then he would say to Simon, "Do you smell that? Do you hear that noise?"

"You're crazy, Jonathan,' Simon laughed.

"No. I really do smell and hear something."

Sometime later, as Jonathan was walking down an avenue between blocks of barracks which housed the prisoners, he began to speak to the Lord:

"What is it Lord?"

In His characteristic way the Lord replied, "My son, the smell you smell is the blood of multitudes which has stained this place and the sound you hear is the cry of innocent blood which ascends to Me for vengeance. The day of vengeance is soon coming. Men have spurned My Grace; they will see My vengeance."

Jonathan's mind was quickly propelled to the Word. It was awesome. God had said to Cain, "The voice of thy brother's blood crieth unto me from the ground," and He was saying that the day of vengeance was soon. It was no wonder that when Jesus read of Himself from Isaiah's scroll, He did not read, "and the day of vengeance of our God," because God in Christ had not come to avenge but now the hour glass was fast running out.

It was the last afternoon in Poland. There was one final drop to make for onward delivery to Russia. Having reached the town at lunchtime there was plenty of time to make the drop and leave Poland. The visas expired that day and the next destination was East Germany - the "creme" of communism. The only problem was that the contact was not at home. The hours dragged on. By four in the afternoon the contact still was not available. A dilemma struck Simon and Jonathan; should they stay and risk severe visa infringement or continue with the literature and deliver it in East Germany. One last effort to make contact was unfruitful. It was decided to leave: the literature was well stowed and they would assuredly get through East German formalities without a problem.

Jonathan was driving. He stopped at a large circle to look at some strange architecture and slowly pulled away. Suddenly there was a squeal of brakes and thump! A small Polish vehicle came seemingly out of nowhere and hit their vehicle denting the front fender. There was no serious damage to either vehicle. The man was shouting and furious: he had to get to Warsaw and it was eight hours journey. Now he would never make it....

Jonathan felt sick. "Why Lord - you could so easily have undertaken. Look - there's plenty of room on either side of me. That car could have gone in front or behind!"

"I have undertaken My son. Agree with thine adversary while you are in the way with Him. I am watching over you - be at peace."

It was over an hour before the police arrived. It took them another hour to get down all the details and give Jonathan a two thousand zlote fine (about $15) for failing to give way. Then, they stamped the visas and informed Jonathan and Simon that they should report to the Insurance next morning. They were cleared to spend one more night in Poland and found a simple country hotel. Early next morning Jonathan and Simon unscrewed the seats and paneling in the vehicle and removed all the hidden literature. They zoomed off for another attempt and were excited to find their contact had arrived home. What a relief and what rejoicing as they unloaded the precious cargo. The car was so much lighter that it felt as if it were floating. At the same time, it seemed as if an incredible weight had lifted off Jonathan and Simon.

"Imagine Simon - if we hadn't' had that accident we would never have delivered those Bibles and that literature."

"I suppose you're saying it's God and not your careless driving?"

"Well actually I do believe that God has a significant hand in what happened - time will reveal it." Simon was quite angry with Jonathan and so the discussion abruptly ended.

The East German border was the most intimidating of all. There was a real hostility as the vehicle pulled up and was directed to a sheltered bay. Immediately it was "pounced upon" and surrounded by guards and shepherd dogs which circled the vehicle sniffing. It was very unnerving but with a show of calm, Jonathan and Simon moved into the office. A tough looking woman immigration officer and a miserable short man with a nasal twine demanded, "Dokumenta." Nobody really appeared to speak English. Jonathan knew they were in trouble mostly because the man was so short and fat and he and Simon were both over six feet. The little man felt threatened and was going to react and react he did!

"Everything. Bring everything," he shouted and continued barking orders to the soldiers outside. There was a flurry of activity as suitcases were unloaded and carried to the office.

While Simon remained inside Jonathan went out to observe the proceedings. Guards were pulling out the seats, unscrewing the panels of the vehicle, checking the wheels, running huge mirrors underneath the vehicle, checking the gas tank. The entire investigation was done under the most oppressive silence. Every suitcase, bag and box of groceries was taken into the office where even sealed cans of meat were subject to X-ray investigation.

So that was the famous East German welcome and treatment. The experience quite matched up to the reports!

Jonathan stood smiling knowingly. A thousand praises rose from his heart to God. "You knew all the time didn't you, Lord?"

What a mess they'd have had if it wasn't for the accident. Suddenly Jonathan realized that the adversary was not satan but God Himself in that scripture. God knew what was in store and had directly intervened in their journey the previous day just so that the Bibles could be delivered. It wasn't pleasant at the time and seemed a real hindrance to the journey but God had solidly shut the door on their proceeding that day. What a disaster it would have become: the East Germans would certainly have found everything and who knows where it might all have ended - a prison cell no doubt.

But as it was, the Germans found nothing. Having put the car together again, the guards smiled and in perfect English said,

"Good-bye, have a pleasant journey." All the time they had been waiting for Jonathan and Simon to betray themselves by speaking something in English to each other. Indeed the ways of the enemy are subtle and devious. It was these same hostile East Germans who had come to Zimbabwe on invitation of the new communist regime there to train the secret police of Zimbabwe; the hated and dreaded CIO which arbitrarily imprisoned, tortured and killed. They were a law unto themselves much like the commanders of Tongogara had been.

CHAPTER TEN

CRY BELOVED LAND

Mocambique, situated on the south east coast of Africa, was settled and colonized by the Portuguese some five hundred years ago. For those five hundred years, Mocambique was an isolated country tied exclusively to mother Portugal politically, socially, economically and religiously.
Evangelism had been strictly forbidden, the Church of Rome holding a powerful monopoly of social, political and religious affairs which she jealously guarded. During the Rusitu Revival of 1906 evangelists from Southern Rhodesia had entered into Mocambique with the Gospel only to be beaten, imprisoned and even killed. Rome was not about to open her doors to the heretics. A protracted struggle against colonial rule which began in the early 1960's, abruptly ended in 1974 when a new socialist government took power in Portugal and gave immediate independence, without regard or forethought to her Portuguese colonies.
FRELIMO (Front for the Liberation of Mocambique) under their Marxist leader Samora Machel took control in Mocambique and immediately instituted a reign of terror upon the citizens both poor and rich alike. A wealthy entrepreneur friend of Jonathan's slashed the antique paintings out of their frames in his luxury mansion and fled. His wife couldn't leave without her jewelry had turned back to snatch her box. As she came out of the bedroom the communist soldiers entered the front door and shot her dead. Another industrialist whom Jonathan came to know simply walked out of his factory never to return. He had managed to smuggle out his wife beforehand. He informed his servants to prepare a dinner party for that evening while he took his smallest and oldest vehicle and headed for the South African border, leaving behind his money, his mansion, his machines and everything that belonged to him.
Nobody was exempt from investigation. All personal property was seized and became the immediate possession of the state for redistribution. People were massacred in their thousands while

others were sent to prisons and asylums and huge slave labor farms so characteristic of the communist system. Mocambique had its own horrendous "Gulag" and the East Germans were invited to set up their secret police system in Mocambique where the "Stassi" equivalent was known as "SNASPS." Like all secret police and intelligence, SNASPS had superiority over any other branch of the forces or government. They were a typical Nazi type "SS," who beat, raped, tortured and exterminated at will and without accountability to anyone.

The whole land became a living hell: nobody was safe, nobody owned anything and everybody belonged to the state. Travel within the country was strictly forbidden except with special passes issued by the Provincial Governors. Everybody was under suspicion for everything or nothing. Materially and economically their communist masters from East Berlin, Prague, Bucharest, Moscow and Havana raped the once rich and thriving country. They pillaged the fish-rich Mocambican channel and plundered the prawn and lobster beds in return for obsolete military equipment. What a joke it was to see old Soviet transistor radios from World War II and fifteen year old tanks sitting in the African jungle - no diesel to operate them and even if there was diesel nobody competent to operate them. In return they took potatoes, oranges, maize, coconuts and cashews. The East Germans seized all the high-grade coal and shipped it home.

The whole state of the land could be summed up in the anecdote of a once thriving cotton mill:

"If they had the workers to run the mill they still couldn't run because there was no electricity. If there had been electricity they still couldn't run because the machines were broken and they didn't have parts. But, if the machines were running they still couldn't operate because there was no cotton. There was no cotton because they couldn't irrigate the fields. If they could have irrigated, the cotton still would not have grown because there was no fertilizer and there was no fertilizer because there were no tractors to haul it. If there were tractors, there were no parts to fix them and they were broken. Even if there were tractors there were no drivers, no laborers to load the fertilizer, no workers to work the fields or pick the cotton - why? Everybody was in prison!"

Ideology can never supersede realism and realism is bread on the table, clothes to wear, a house in which to live and peace. Jesus is the greatest realist that has ever lived.

By 1980 Mocambique's Samora Machel and his Marxist cronies had become an embarrassment even to many within their own FRELIMO party. A breakaway group had formed under the name RENAMO (Resistencia Nacionale Mocambican) to fight the excesses of communism and introduce a democratic system of government. And so Mocambique experienced the compounded problem of a serious civil war as well as the ravages of communism.

It was into this beaten, bruised and bleeding nation that the Holy Spirit called Jonathan giving him a special love for her. The country was well known to Jonathan as his family had always spent their vacations there. This had abruptly ended in the 1974 take-over. From 1982 Jonathan made countless sorties into Mocambique, smuggling in Bibles and literature, preaching and teaching in the underground churches, establishing leaders and generally encouraging those who had suffered so much under the appalling communism. Some highlights of those victories - because even apparent defeats with God are victories if walking in His perfect will - are both stirring and amusing.

It was the midday heat of midsummer. The soldiers and border guards lay around in the shade dozing or idly chatting. There was a foul smell of spent excrement oozing from the long overflowing latrines. The flush had ceased to work in 1975 but the toilet continued to be used and cleaned out every now and then with a shovel - a little less now than then! Fat bulging blue bottle maggot flies buzzed noisily as they went to deposit their loads of maggots attracted by the foul odor that seemed to cling to the very clothes that Jonathan wore.

"Boa tarde," (good afternoon) said Jonathan to an apathetic guard who looked him up and down with disdain. There were neither immigration nor customs officers present.

"Siesta - a tres, mais ou menos (At three, more or less)."

"T.I.A. (this is Africa)." said Jonathan, "a very far cry from East Germany."

The wait was a long one. Jonathan was very amused at the total lack of discipline amongst the soldiers and wondered what would happen if there was an attack. The heat was oppressive, the flies annoying. At two o'clock the officials arrived and having paid the necessary dues and had passports stamped they came for a "look" at the vehicle. What a search: it was every bit as thorough as East Germany but the Bibles were well secure and hidden in drums of diesel as there was no diesel to be had in the country and they had to carry their own. The back of the pick-up contained five drums - one with water, two with diesel and two with Bibles, literature and other vital supplies for the believers. The men were finally softened with a couple of cokes and Jonathan with his interpreter, Jeremiah, were released for their journey to Beira, second largest city of Mocambique.

There were twenty-six roadblocks between the border and Beira, a distance of only one hundred and sixty miles. It was quite possible for the soldiers to force a person to unload the vehicle at each roadblock. It did not take much to upset the gun-happy soldiers: a wrong comment or simply the look on a face could detain a person at their pleasure for as long as they wished. Jonathan who had traveled the route several times found that soap was an incredible incentive. Most people had not seen soap in years and it was like gold dust. One time some senior commanders begged Jonathan for coke. On that particular trip he was carrying several liter bottles. He gladly offered the coke but insisted on keeping the empty bottles. No problem (nao problema) - a brand new mortar container was summoned, the mortar bomb thrown out into the sand and the coke poured into the container. That was coke with zest! As they arrived at the first roadblock, Jonathan waved at the soldiers and started passing out the soap before the pick-up even stopped. There were yells and shouts and laughter as the men opened the barrier and waved on the travelers. Nothing was certain however. Those soldiers were totally unpredictable: one day they would laugh with you, the next just as soon cut your throat and for no reason. Many travelers had had their entire possessions robbed from them at gunpoint and forced to watch as it was shamelessly distributed. Others had actually been shot at the roadblocks... it was only the mercy and saving grace of the Almighty that kept Jonathan on such journeys.

Needless to say, progress on those journeys was very slow. Anything could be lurking in the dense tropical bush that had encroached upon the roads for lack of upkeep. There was no money for road works. It was hard to believe the dilapidation of towns and villages in seven short years of Marxism. Marxist slogans and graffiti covered every available wall. Communist monuments and the typical Red Star were in every town square. It was always the "year" of the workers but the workers had no work. Most were in slave labor camps or prisons. Once prosperous companies were closed; windows smashed, graffiti on the walls, machinery and equipment lying rusting outside, exposed to every element. Every Roman church or cathedral was either locked with huge chains and padlocks or had been commandeered by the local militia or had become dance halls. It was amusing but tragic to see tanks sitting on a hill surrounding one simple radio mast. Everywhere was the marks of oppression, suffering and fear. Like Eastern Europe, nobody smiled and everybody expected every one to be a spy for SNASPS or an informer.

There was a marked absence of domestic animals. For three years after "independence" FRELIMO had embarked on a binge of continuous eating and drinking. The breweries had finally run out and closed operations, livestock were systematically slaughtered to feed all and sundry - national herds were decimated; chicken, pig and cattle breeders were cleaned out. The only domestic animals not touched were the dogs which had become lean and mean "tick taxis" with their putrefying sores and their "skin stretched-over-ribs," bodies.

A huge supermarket might contain some cheap paraffin (kerosene) lamps from China, some old packets of tea, a few cheap cotton dresses and the joke of jokes, hundreds of rolls of toilet paper. Food was never seen on the shelves and the only place to buy anything was at special "Intafranca" shops which catered for the Russian, East German, and Cuban marauders. Imported goods at exorbitant prices could be purchased with only hard currency. The irony was that hard currency was British Pounds, West German Marks and good old U.S. dollars.

It was seven as Jonathan and Jeremiah reached the cordon which surrounded Beira. The whole city was surrounded by a enormous military cordon initially to prevent attack from the west but more latterly as protection against RENAMO "terrorists" or "bandits" as they were called. Their documents were thoroughly scrutinized and the vehicle searched. The drums were legitimate as everyone knew there was no diesel and no drinking water in the city. Having been cleared, the huge barrier was lifted and the pick-up proceeded into the ghost city of Beira. There were no street or shop lights. What little power existed was preserved for the equally little industry. Large generators lighted the Russian compound. There were no restaurants in service and only two hotels operating. Jonathan had stayed at the old elite Ambassador Hotel the previous journey. There was no running water and no power. Water from the slimy swimming pool was carried in buckets up the stairs for toilet and bathing. Jonathan had taken one of the old beautiful cut glass crystal ornamental lamps and filled it with diesel from his vehicle to give some lighting. Two candles lighted the magnificent big dining room. The "chef" offered rancid pork and rice on the menu and one bottle of beer per customer. What a dinner in a supposed five star hotel.

That night however, Jonathan and Jeremiah were staying in the home of the Beira Port Captain whose wife was a believer and himself very sympathetic. The state had given them a palatial home befitting his position and they loved to entertain Jonathan and were comfortably able since visiting ships always well provisioned the captain. Jonathan often felt that the welcome he was afforded must have been how the early Christians under similar conditions of persecution received Paul.

It was a graceful home in the elite suburbs and not far from the Governor's mansion. At least there would be running water and quite possibly power though Jonathan had brought his gas equipment including his gas deep freeze with meat and dairy provisions. How well he remembered being invited to the home of another saintly lady. She was so excited to have them that she had sacrificed her most precious and meager meat ration for them. The only problem was the meat was already green and rotten. Nevertheless, Jonathan had prayed a double blessing and eaten with grace. He didn't relish that experience again.

Mathilda and Augustino welcomed the men with great enthusiasm and much chatting. How good the Lord had been and Mathilda was full of what God had been doing amongst the believers. Some of the pastors had been released from prison though they had been badly tortured and "Pastor," she added, "the people are going to be blessed you have come. We never expected you. What a surprise..."

"Always so gracious Mathilda," Jonathan said. "Look, Jeremiah has to go and make some other contacts. He insists tonight. He's actually twisted my arm into letting him use the Peugeot. I must be getting soft or stupid or both. Don't bother to stow the vehicle as he will be taking off shortly."   "First we must eat and fellowship and then Jeremiah can go," Mathilda laughed.

"Pastor, Pastor, it's six o'clock and Jeremiah did not come back. I'm very worried. No phone, nothing." For Mathilda to worry meant things were not good.

"I don't even know where he went Mathilda: not a single name. He refused to say and since he's not a novice, I left the subject alone. There's nothing to do but pray. At least he might call. He has your number."

Jonathan was still in prayer when the 'phone rang.

"Jeremiah where are you? What's happened?... Yes I know it. Yes, yes. But you better speak to Jonathan... No... Okay, I'll tell him. Bye."

"What is it Mathilda, what happened to Jeremiah?"

Mathilda looked very sheepish as she said, "You'll never believe this but last night Jeremiah thought that he didn't have enough diesel so he stopped to..."

"Oh no, and in the dark he filled the tank from the water drum," interrupted Jonathan. "The idiot. Where's he now?"

"He was too ashamed to tell you...."

" That's very fine. In this country under these conditions? He could have been in prison for all we knew..." anguished Jonathan.

"The place is clear across town. There are no buses and no taxis but I have a friend who could take you there during lunch hour. You cannot possible walk - besides, it's too much exposure. You shouldn't been seen too openly."

"I knew, I knew, I knew! I should never have let him use the pick-up. Did he start the engine after adding the water? If he did we have a very big job."

"That I don't know, Pastor. Problem is that there are no mechanics to trust. They will rob all your parts especially a diesel pick-up," cautioned Mathilda.

It was a long and frustrating wait but finally Jose da Silva arrived in a beat up old Ford Cortina, the kind with paint peeling off, windows that did not wind shut and a piece of foam cushion to cover the exposed seat springs. Jonathan smiled and recalled what he had often told the natives, "a third class ride is better than a first class walk." The amazing tale that Jose told was that he was quite often free at lunch because there was nothing to eat. In fact he only ate once every second evening because there was simply nothing available, "and many" he added, "Are in the same situation."

It was immediately evident on their arrival at the Peugeot that Jeremiah had indeed started the engine. Water was in everything - injectors, pipes, filters and it entailed a major stripping and cleaning process. Jonathan did not relish the thought of the vehicle being another night on that road. He quietly rejoiced that he had brought along his entire toolbox. It was a long process of elimination until everything had been cleaned and washed with the precious supply of diesel. They worked feverishly to put everything together again and by six o'clock they were ready to start the engine. No life! They needed a tow and flagged down an old Landrover. He obliged for a price - everything was for a price. Finally the pick-up sputtered to life and after some fine adjustments she was running smoothly.

It seemed so routine but there was always the fear of being discovered by SNASP. Jonathan was on a transit visa to Malawi. In those days it was the only way to get into Mocambique. To be discovered on a transit visa would have meant instant arrest. It always seemed like any official government vehicle that passed by as they worked in silence would scream out, "There they are! Look! Get them!" Mocambique was tough and those communists were not playing. They were afraid of everything and everyone - the West, spies, C.I.A., RENAMO, South Africa. They arrested or shot first and then asked questions. Nobody was safe and nobody was above the Godless system. In fact, God was enemy number one and their rhetoric was supported by their actions.

There were State registered churches. They received visitors and Bibles and occupied the best old cathedrals. Their pastors were slick and fat. There were all the form of godliness but absolutely no power. The underground churches met in basements and shacks on the outskirts of town. They met in warehouses and old disused factories. They baptized in the mangrove swamps and it was in the mangroves that the best meetings took place.

It was a Robin Hood affair. The mangroves were inland swamps matted with trees and vines and alive with the most incredible creatures. There were bright colored lizards with fish-like tails, frogs and snakes. There were insects of every kind and color and of course mosquitoes, mosquitoes, mosquitoes!! And, the mangroves stank. But, unless a person knew their way in and out of them the mangroves would swallow up an entire army. They were a fortress of security and one wrong turn took one to disaster. On small islands in the midst of the mangroves the believers built simple churches. It was there that they could dance and praise and worship and baptize in mangrove ponds in the midst of the security and secrecy afforded by nature. The believers who gathered in this fashion were like the Albigensians and Monrovians who kept the standard of Jesus flying in a depraved and corrupted world. To these saints belong the laurel wreaths for their uncompromising stand and faithfulness to the call, the true martyrs who laid down their all, many even their lives to keep the fires burning.

The following week was exciting if not dangerous. There was always SNASP to be avoided, secret meetings to attend and assisting the local pastors with teaching and encouragement. The pastors declared, "We don't need things. We've learned to do without even food. But Pastor, we know you love us because you have bothered to come. Please keep coming and tell our friends overseas to come. They don't have to bring anything, just come." How humbling in the face of their poverty and suffering to see their stoicism and love for the Lord. There were pastors, elders and members who could show the marks of Christ: there were the cruel beatings and one pastor had lost an eye, others were maimed and loved ones imprisoned all for the Gospel. With silent bearing of their cross these saints of the hidden churches radiated the glory of a risen, living, dynamic Jesus. What joy and victory was each meeting and there invaded a powerful presence of the Holy Spirit into those mud and thatch churches in the mangroves.

The Peugeot pick-up always seemed out of place amidst the Russian and East German armored carriers. FRELIMO soldiers and police infested the city; of course, there was nothing to buy and no entertainment except the sea and sand. All the animals in the famous zoo had been killed and eaten; there were no films at the movie houses, no clubs, restaurants or hotels catering for off-duty soldiers. There were no tourists.

Jonathan and Jeremiah always tried to be inconspicuous and traveled during afternoon siesta or early evening before it became dark. The vehicle was always locked in Mathilda's garage at night because of both thieves and investigation. After a week of ministering and encouraging the believers it was time for Jonathan and Jeremiah to proceed the 450 miles to the city of Tete on the famous Zambezi River.

The journey to Tete included a 200-mile section called "ambush alley". Before the road was finally closed by RENAMO, people traveled at their own risk. Every few miles there were burned out vehicles from ambushes and huge craters from landmines. Jonathan well remembers on a previous trip with Jeremiah stopping to look at the engine of a burned-out landcruiser. They were stopped about halfway down ambush alley. There was a breeze that rustled the trees. Suddenly someone shouted, "a vehicle," but then everything seemed so silent again. Jonathan and Dick, a missionary who was with him and Jeremiah on that trip, continued to inspect the vehicle when suddenly there appeared over the brow of the hill a FRELIMO armored troop carrier bristling with soldiers. CAUGHT! "O God, help us," they breathed.

Soldiers leaped from the vehicle in all directions hitting the ground and rolling over into the bush. Within seconds there were rockets, mortars, machine guns and A.K. rifles trained on the missionaries and their vehicle. Jonathan and Dick threw up their hands in the "surrender' pose. They were tense moments as the missionaries expected an avalanche of missiles to assail them. After some considerable time of heart racing and sweat pouring, the missionaries were motioned to proceed cautiously towards the FRELIMO truck. Dick slowly drove while Jonathan walked beside the vehicle with his hands up. Jeremiah was seated in the back of the pick-up.

The relief of the soldiers that they were not in an ambush was as great as the relief of the missionaries that they had not been splattered over the road. Relief brought hysterical laughter all round and missionaries and soldiers laughed together in ambush alley. The soldiers in the armored vehicle were also relieved that the missionaries, coming from the opposite direction had reached that far in safety as it meant the road would be open for them.

Waving and laughing the missionaries beat a hasty retreat before the unpredictable soldiers changed their minds and began asking too many questions or decided to arrest them.

Jonathan and Jeremiah laughed and chatted as they remembered the incident while passing the spot. The landcrusier still lay in the bush as testimony to the encounter. What an escape it had been.

"You know Jeremiah, it is amazing how peaceful it is out here in the midst of all this war. I get so excited I want to dance and shout and laugh all at the same time. It's God...."

"You crezeee Pastor, I know you crezeee. To come here on this road alone. I hate it,' interjected Jeremiah.

"Then why do you come if you're so afraid?" inquired Jonathan.

"Well....Well....it's because....it's because," stammered Jeremiah.

"It's because you know very well that God is always with us. The problem with you black Africans is that you are ruled by fear even when you see the reality of victory. But I must admire your courage that in spite of your fear you still come. Or," continued Jonathan "is it because you love me and you just hate it when I'm away? You're afraid you're missing something?"

"Not that," laughed Jeremiah who betrayed himself with a blush that turned his black face even blacker.

"Well I don't know why I bring you anyway," interjected Jonathan. "Look at the trouble you cause me."

"Maybe it's because you love me too," shot back Jeremiah with the whites of his eyes rolling. Jonathan laughed and closed the subject with, "You're deceived pal," but Jeremiah had that knowing look.

It was late afternoon as they sped along ambush alley. The sun was fast sinking in the western sky and its watery rays filtered through the stark trees along the road. Bushes and elephant grass had grown into the road narrowing the paving to an almost single lane. Each bend was a perfect spot for an ambush or landmine. The grass was tall and tawny, leonine in color. It was winter and everything was dry. There was always an excitement in the air of what might happen. Jonathan kept his ear tuned to the murmuring of the diesel engine: especially after the episode of the water. It was no place to break down in ambush alley which was literally hundreds of miles from civilization. Besides which, even if one reached the nearest town there would be no spares. This was communist Mocambique in war: certainly not a place to procure vehicle spares. The road was conspicuously deserted even of wild game and birds. Jonathan wondered what might be lurking in the bush. Little did he know that one day he would be in that same bush watching ambush alley instead of driving it. They had spent a long and very tiring day on the road. With all the roadblocks, questions and tensions, Jonathan and Jeremiah were quite drained by the time they reached Tete. It was dark and cold as they made for a small park along the banks of the mighty Zambezi River. This was the very town from which David Livingstone had set sail for England almost a hundred years before. It had also been the center for the southern African slave trade. The Arab slavers sailed their dhows up the Zambezi as far as Tete to take on their slave cargoes and off load salt, cloth, beads and other such items. Tete was the last navigable point on the Zambezi, 150 miles inland from the Indian Ocean. It is a hot, humid, mosquito-infested town for most of the year and the only bridge crossing of the Zambezi River in 500 miles. It was from Tete that Livingstone launched his attack on the slave trade of Central Africa which ended in Queen Victoria's annexation of vast territories for no other reason than to stamp out the hated slavery.

Jonathan and Jeremiah rolled out their ground sheets, laid out sleeping bags and blankets and covered over with another large ground sheet to prevent being soaked by the frost which often fell in mid-winter. They ate a scanty meal, collapsed into bed and fell into a deep sleep. Jonathan was so tired he passed out. The Holy Spirit tried to awaken him several times and in his subconscious he knew something to be seriously wrong be he just couldn't seem to pull himself together and awake. He was dreaming the strangest things. Jonathan only dreamed when it was from God and God was calling, God was warning, God was attempting to arouse His servant.

A scream and shouting pierced the night air. Jonathan emerged from sleep like a man coming out of anesthesia. It was odd. He never slept like that, no matter how tired. As the shouting continued, Jonathan leapt to his feet. Jeremiah was gone. He heard him shouting down the road and then there was silence. Jonathan ran off in the direction from which the shouting had come to find Jeremiah writhing in agony on the ground with blood pouring from his mouth and head. He was moaning and groaning.

"O Lord, he's been stabbed," muttered Jonathan. "And here in Tete. What are we going to do?" Jonathan carried him back to the pick-up. Jeremiah was obviously in a state of shock and near unconsciousness. He was mumbling, "Get me to the hospital. Get me to the hospital."

"Jeremiah, you know you cannot go to the hospital. There's no medicine and even if there were they'd arrest you before they gave you any," said Jonathan.

Jeremiah decided if he couldn't get to a hospital he was going to die. The biggest problem with that is that when a native decides he's going to die, he dies. Jonathan had horrendous visions of trying to get Jeremiah back to Zimbabwe - past all the roadblocks, police, customs, immigration and whatever else. He had visions of Jeremiah dead but propped up like a man who was too sick to move.

"Please Lord, You can do it," whispered Jonathan, "You can take care of this situation."

"I'm dying, Pastor, I'm dying. Find me a doctor," groaned Jeremiah.

"I cannot. Not here in Tete," said Jonathan. "I've got good medicine and I know how to use it."
"I'm dying. What about my wife and kids?" he mumbled.
Jonathan raced to get the medicines. "You'll be all right, I promise you,' said Jonathan. "I'll get you back to Zimbabwe tomorrow."
There were no stab wounds on Jeremiah but Jonathan feared there might be some internal injuries as natives are particularly weak in their solar plexus if hit in that particular spot. What Jonathan could piece together was that thieves had come and were stealing whatever they could find. Jeremiah had awakened to see them making off with his suitcase. He'd given chase, tripped over his own pants and had gone flying head first into a wall.
Jonathan cleaned up the superficial wounds and gave Jeremiah a shot of morphine to knock him out. He cradled him for a while until he passed out before piling blankets on top of him to keep him warm. Jeremiah had slurred off, "I'm dying pastor, I'm dying." Jonathan knew that their trip was over. He would have to get Jeremiah back to Zimbabwe to a doctor on the morrow. He sat back with a cup of coffee he'd made and began to think of what had happened. It troubled him that he'd not woken because this was a war zone and Jonathan was used to war and usually very alert.
"Why Lord? What happened?" questioned Jonathan.
"They put you to sleep my son," whispered the Lord. They had knives and machetes and were going to kill you but I said "NO." I allowed them to take your things but not your life. You are mine. Nobody can touch you; nobody can have you. You are mine. Now, check your suitcase," commanded the Lord. Sure enough, only a pair of socks remained - everything had been taken, except our lives.
"What a deliverance Lord. You saved my life. Thank You. Thank You," exclaimed Jonathan.
"My pleasure, My son. I love you," declared the Lord.
"I love you too Lord," replied Jonathan.
Next morning at first light they returned to Zimbabwe.

CHAPTER ELEVEN

MISSION IMPOSSIBLE

Nao visa, nao go," slurred the lazy, half-drunk immigration officer in his tattered blue uniform. It was hard enough and dangerous enough for Zimbabweans to go into Mocambique but Jonathan was now taking some Americans. If anything went wrong, they would all be arrested on the grounds the Americans were C.I.A. agents. Not a pleasant situation.

The customs house was dirty with mud splattered up the walls. Communist slogans had been daubed everywhere and in the office hung faded and tattered posters heralding the glories and "Year of the Worker." Both were lies. It was always the year of the worker. Tubu was a remote outpost in a dry, hot and dusty land. By 10.00 a.m. the temperatures were already reaching 105°. Communist soldiers with worn and faded camouflage outfits from East Germany were slouched over their AK rifles. One lay snoring on the porch, the flies buzzing noisily around him. He was totally oblivious to them or the vehicles of the visitors who had arrived. The customs officer had lost interest in the affairs of the seven travelers and left his post to join his dice-playing friends outside. Jonathan was left with Jeremiah in the office. He looked around quickly and saw the "ENTRY" stamp lying on the desk. His mind raced. "Jeremiah go outside and keep those men talking," he whispered.

'I don't like this," Jeremiah questioned, "you're up to something Pastor?"

Jonathan was already out of the door and to the car. Slipping on his jacket with its big pockets he instructed Pete to gather all passports. Of course, one of the team had to shout out, "What are you doing with that jacket on in this incredible heat?" Jonathan acted as if he never heard, slid into the customs house, crawled under the counter and grabbed the stamp off the desk. Slipping it into his pocket he slipped out of the building again. He could see the soldiers, customs and immigration officials slouching outside and there were no other visitors trying to pass through. Time was important. Should he get caught it would be prison at best; probably a bullet. This was war. These men did not have to explain anything if they shot someone. There were really accountable to nobody and Jonathan was used to their whims. They were so unpredictable: one moment they were friendly and the very next they could take your possessions, intimidate you or lock you up. Jonathan grabbed the passports from Pete and shoved them into his other pocket. He casually walked around to ensure that nobody's suspicions were aroused and once satisfied he ambled off to the back of the customs house. There was an old disused office with papers strewn on the floor. Piles of old human feces turned his stomach but it was the perfect place. Anyone who might have seen him enter the office would think he'd gone in for the same reason.... Shelves lined the walls. Jonathan placed the passports on the shelves and quickly stamped them one by one on the appropriate page. Each time the stamp hit a passport with the characteristic "Wham, click" it was as if the whole world was shouting "In here," "get him!" Sweat was pouring off Jonathan's face from both the heat and the excitement. He knew very well that without the stamp carrying its picture of a little motorcar it would be impossible for the team to travel within the country. At every roadblock the soldiers wanted to see that picture. Most of them couldn't read a word but they would always recognize the little green vehicle on the stamp and that was sufficient. It was official. At any moment an official or soldier might come along. Jonathan stopped to listen after every "wham, click" of the stamp. Nothing! Finishing the last passport he quickly stuffed them into one pocket and the stamp into the other. Nonchalantly he walked back towards the office. What seemed like hours were barely a couple of minutes. Jonathan thought, "I cannot believe I'm doing this. Only for You, Lord," he whispered.

Everybody was in the exact position they'd been and Jeremiah had become the center of attention. He'd engaged everyone in an entertaining story and Jonathan knew that Jeremiah had caught on to what was happening. Jonathan entered the customs building again. Still nobody was around. Quickly he hit the floor, crawled under the counter and replaced the stamp in its exact position. A radio was blaring native music from the vacant office of the local controller. He too was enthralled with Jeremiah's story. Jonathan slipped from the office and slowly moved towards the car. He took off the sweat-soaked jacket containing the precious passports and dropped it on the seat. As calmly as possible Jonathan strolled up to the group and mingled on the edge for a while. There were soldiers everywhere. Why hadn't they seen? Why hadn't they followed? Did somebody know and was he waiting for an opportunity? After a while Jonathan announced, "Well, it's time to be going. It's a long way back to Harare..." Turning to the Immigration Officer he informed him, "We will return without the Americans tomorrow."

"Si, Si, senhor. For you, nao problema. Americana nao bo, nao bo." (No good, no good).

Everybody laughed, shook hands and patted backs in true Portuguese style. Jonathan couldn't wait to leave. The team was bursting to know what was happening.

"I'll explain after we get into Zims," declared Jonathan. "Let's just clear Customs and Immigration back there first." It was amazing how different the spirit was by simply crossing the border. Even although Zimbabwe too, had embraced Marxism, it was somewhat freer and there was a good commercial and industrial network. Over a Coke at the local gas station Jonathan explained, "we'll not go back to Harare. We'll camp up for the day - there's a dam twenty miles back. Tonight we'll come back to the border and I'll lead Pete, Riga and Babs across. Jeremiah, Dick, and Trish will follow with the vehicles tomorrow. We'll hide up about a mile from the customs post inside Mocambique. When you leave the customs Dick and Trish, you'll honk your horns. I'll scatter stones in the road and put some rocks beside the road so you'll know where we are. Stop immediately and we'll get into the vehicles and be on our way. The passports are stamped so we'll have no problem getting around once inside the country."

Everybody began to chatter excitedly but it was Jeremiah who was not happy. He didn't like it, didn't think they should go, didn't think it was God's will. The problem was that his Tete affair was still too fresh in his mind. He was being typically ruled by fear and Jonathan knew deep down that the best thing was to give a Gideon order - "all who are afraid, go home..." but Jeremiah was both their guide and interpreter.

"Well Jeremiah, we're actually in this situation because you failed to organize properly and to do your job..." rebuked Jonathan. "What else do you want to do? So far, everything you've suggested has been a disaster, Jeremiah."

"All right," declared Jeremiah, "but the Bible says we're not supposed to tempt God and this is tempting God."

Jonathan was used to that statement - he'd heard it so many times from Christians who always refused to face up to the real reasons they would not do something in the service of the Lord.

"Of course it's dangerous, Jeremiah, but no more so or ridiculous than Jonathan and his armor bearer going up against the camp of the Philistines. God is big. You of all people should know that. Come on man, stop being full of 'maybe's, ifs and buts' and let's do something for Jesus. Don't quit now...." continued Jonathan.

"Well, I just don't like it. It's ridiculous...."

"Yea Jeremiah, many things that God's people did in the Bible were ridiculous," interjected Babs.

"Okay, I'm not for democracy but here's the situation," continued Jonathan. "If something goes wrong and we're caught then the visitors will be expelled, Dick and Trish should be safe so it'll be Jeremiah and I who land up in Chikurubi. Who's for us proceeding?"

Everybody chorused an "AMEN" while Jeremiah threw stones dejectedly. He was not really with the team as they made off towards the dam for the day.

It was October and suicide month again. The temperatures were undoubtedly in the 120 degrees, the tar was sticky, the sun blazing and sweat pouring. Jeremiah had a pastor friend he wanted to visit. It was very like him: he knew people everywhere.

"I'll cycle over to the dam about 6 o'clock so that we can be ready to go," he said.

"Don't be late Jeremiah," instructed Jonathan, "I do not want hassles of having to search for you. This is serious business."

"Yes Pastor. Bye." He waved as he closed the door of the old 1965 Mercedes, "See you at six."

"Well," said Riga, "that's the last we'll see of Jeremiah. He'll not come."

"Oh I don't know," replied Pete, "let's trust God..." Pete was a smallish man with a thick beard and rather soft voice. He was somewhat wimpish and clearly under the domination of his overbearing wife, Riga, and her ministry assistant, Babs. They'd often have to gather for "councils of peace" as they called them but Jonathan always figured that Pete got a lickin' each and every time. He was often withdrawn and seemed quite happy being alone although Jonathan suspected it to be a tactic of self-defense. Babs who always sided with Riga cut him short in his opinion.

"Riga's right Pete. Jeremiah's a coward. He'll not be going with us tonight...."

"I saw his type many times in communist East Germany.... You can never trust them," shrilled Riga, "you can never trust them. They always let you down."

"So what will we do if Jeremiah doesn't show Jonathan?" questioned Pete.

"Proceed as scheduled. I know more about Mocambique than Jeremiah - in fact I introduced him to the country. It's only the language but God can raise up someone for that..." replied Jonathan confidently.

"Why sure," injected Riga, "we came all the way for this and things are starting to get fun. Jonathan's my kind... let's go for it," she declared.

"I love it," chorused Babs.

Pete had already immersed himself in some novel knowing that his opinion didn't account for too much and that he could not be relied upon....

"Wow," mused Jonathan silently to himself, "together with Trish it makes quite a Jezebel team.... It kinda leaves Dick and me but then Dick will always do what Trish relay wants.... Hey, Lord HELP! How did I get into this mess?" Jonathan had drifted off into fellowship with the Lord who was distinctly chuckling at Jonathan's predicament and simply said as only He can,

"Have fun My son...."

Jonathan smiled and replied, "typically you, Lord," which he spoke aloud but nobody was listening. Pete was into his book while Babs and Riga were chattering excitedly like a couple of chipmunks. Dick and Trish followed the old Merc in the ministry's equally old Peugeot pick-up loaded with equipment and towing a trailer with supplies. The dam was picturesque and the team set up camp for the day under some acacia's which spread their umbrella type canopies of shade. It was much cooler in the shade but the hot breeze made it seem as though a huge central heating system had been turned on. Food was not a consideration in this situation and the only solution was to drink plenty of water, stay in the shade and keep covered. Not only was there the very real danger of sunstroke in the blazing rays of the October sun, but also the problem of heat stroke. In no short time, the whole electrolyte system of the body could become dysfunctional, causing headaches, nausea and disorientation. Though Jonathan was a white African he was always very careful when it came the sun. He marveled at how his black counterparts could stand and work all day in such conditions with absolutely no side effects.

Six o'clock finally came with the sun dipping on the western horizon. It would be ten or eleven before it cooled down. Jeremiah was nowhere to be seen and deep in his heart Jonathan knew he'd not be showing. Pete and Dick went on a hunt for him which ended fruitless after a couple of hours. By nine o'clock the team was exhausted and collapsed into fitful sleep. They needed to move out by 1.30 a.m. because it would begin to get light by 4.30 a.m. and Jonathan and team needed to be well secured by twilight. The natives awoke with the sun and they certainly did not need to be spotted dashing through the bush after daybreak. Secretly, Jonathan hoped and prayed that Jeremiah would come during the night hours. He knew only too well the consequences of "desertion" in the army of the Lord. People think that it is a mere question of forgiveness. "It's easy to forgive," said Jonathan later "but the problem of guilt seems to remain. I well remember my team which ran away at the Tongagara crusade in Middle Sabi. Of course I forgave them - I loved them. But they knew they'd ditched me in crisis. Those people never came to terms with that either spiritually or naturally. There was always somewhat of a distance with all of them afterwards. I never loved them any less but it was their guilt that separated us. In later years, they went on to actually betray me. What I feared most about Jeremiah was that he could become very dangerous. We'd done so much underground work together, so much Bible smuggling and knew so many contacts that if the enemy sowed seeds in his heart towards me he would be vulnerable. It's a principle. There was an issue for offense, which could easily lead to his betraying me, and more so because the new communist authorities were opposed to the church and the secret police, the C.I.O. were ruthless. They'd torture Jeremiah for information and it was for all our contacts that I was most concerned and including Jeremiah himself. Judas had been remorseful over Jesus but he never repented: that would have taken a great battle in the spirit. If Judas had repented he would never have hanged himself. That Jeremiah did actually ditch us became a major problem in our relationship. In fact, as I feared at the time we ceased working together and Jeremiah did, in fact give information about me under pressure. "It's tough," choked Jonathan with tears pouring down his cheeks, "but that's how it is. Jeremiah never repented. How much we lose for our wrong decisions. Jeremiah deserted. I well know that desertion in the natural army carried life-imprisonment or even death and correctly so because you endanger the lives of all who rely upon you. Well, I came to realize that desertion in God's army also carries a death sentence. What an enormous price to pay."

Jeremiah did not show. A last search along the way proved fruitless. He'd gone, caught the bus to Harare. Later, at a chance meeting in Mutare, Jeremiah offered a pathetic excuse, I thought without me you would not go...."

"You should have known me better than that," cut in Jonathan. It was the end of a long relationship and it was final as only things like that can be in the spirit.

The night air was finally cool even a little chilly but that might also have been due to anticipated excitement. There were no lights on in Tubu because the only sources of power were generators and in characteristic form, the natives had probably forgotten to order more diesel before the last supplies ran out. Their philosophy is quite simple and Biblical, "why worry about tomorrow? Let the morrow worry about it's own affairs." Such a philosophy was not conducive to heart attacks to be sure and certainly on a night like that, it was a blessing to Jonathan and his party.

They stopped the vehicles a long way from the border post and Jonathan set off to scout. All his old instincts were instantly alerted. Every sensor in his being was activated and ready to sound the alarm if things were not in order. It was a brilliant night. The sky was filled with one of the most wonderful displays of stars Jonathan had ever seen. There was no moon but the whole universe appeared to be well lit. Jonathan did not stop to ponder all the magnificence - there was other business to be done. Quickly and quietly he made his way to the border. His eyes took in every detail: positions of buildings lie of the land, shadows. Above all, he was searching for the patrols or the border guards and the whereabouts of any dogs.

It was quiet. Very quiet. Too quiet in fact. Like a lithe silhouette himself, Jonathan darted from tree shadows to buildings. Stop. Listen. No sounds, no movements. Another quick dart and he reached the fence line and lay low. Again he stopped to listen. Nobody had seen him, nobody had heard. He crawled along the fence until he found the gate. Thank God they had removed the barbed wire and alarms as well as trip wires to anti-personnel mines. He breathed a sigh of relief. The gate was pooled in blackness from a huge tree. Where was the guard though? It worried Jonathan. He wanted to know the exact location of the guard.   He could be awake but just having a smoke break. Jonathan didn't want him poking his nose in at the wrong moment. He quickly cut across the Customs House and dashed around the corner. As if expecting an ambush any moment he slipped along the wall stealthily. Cautiously he peered around the corner. Ah, there it was! The faintly glowing embers of a log from a long-starved fire were lying amidst powdery ashes. The rhythmic snore of a deeply sleeping native sounded from the porch. Jonathan crept around to see. He peered cautiously into the porch. Two guards were completely enshrouded in blankets which made Jonathan happy and a little more confident. He'd found the guards. No weapons either - they had become casual since the war ended and neither were there any dogs. Jonathan whispered an audible prayer, "knock them out Lord. Put such a sleep on them that nothing will awaken them for at least the next four hours." With that he swiftly returned to the vehicle to get the rest of the team. There was no time to waste. Daylight would come altogether too quickly and they needed to be well secured before then.

"Let's go," he whispered, "move out!" Everything's clear but remember do exactly what I say and when I say it." Jonathan had experienced problems with novices and disobedient Christians before and he wasn't ready to have any unnecessary problems because people thought they knew better or didn't want to listen.

"Keep in single file and Pete, you take the rear. Make sure that nothing jangles or knocks as you walk. Absolutely no talking or even whispering and no flashlights whatsoever." There was part of an old minefield they would have to cross and Jonathan cautioned again, "wherever I step, you step! I don't want anyone to set off a mine...."

"Is all this real," squeaked Babs, "I can't believe I'm here. This is the most exciting mission I've been on. You really are a wildman, Jonathan. It seems that everything they said about you is true."

"I don't need to know..." interrupted Jonathan. "Let's get on with our mission. Let's go."

With a final wave to Dick and Trish and a confirmation regarding their rendezvous they all started out with Jonathan in the lead.

They glided like shadows, silently keeping cover at every opportunity. There were some dilapidated buildings near the border gates. Having reached the point safely, Jonathan regrouped and gave the final orders. He had taught the women how to climb the fence and then swing their legs out and wide in a great arc to avoid getting tangled in the barbed wire running along the top. It was a technique and Jonathan felt like an aerobics instructor before the activity ever became popular. This first fence was not too bad and only about nine feet high. Jonathan scaled it in true African style with Babs and Riga following. Pete came up the rear and was the only one to get his pants caught in the wire. The women started to hiss at him but Jonathan motioned absolute silence and instructed them to get low in some grass near the road. Pete really was going to be in trouble when the ban on speaking was lifted. In his predicament there was only one thing do. Jonathan drew his knife and cut Pete's jeans, releasing him from the tangle into which he'd got himself. He almost crashed head over heels from the top of the fence but managed to save himself in time. Jonathan's ears were straining. All noises were magnified in the still morning air. Jonathan fought back the urge to imagine that the whole world was alerted. He looked anxiously towards the Customs House where three guards were sleeping and panicked for a second before remembering the prayer he'd offered up to the Lord concerning keeping them asleep. He relaxed. The whole episode couldn't have lasted more than two minutes but, in two minutes Jonathan had seen men die for similar mistakes. His heart was thumping, the sweat was pouring but finally Pete was down. He'd tried his best but Riga and Babs were hostile and he really was intimidated by them which is probably why he messed up.

A dog began to yooowl near the Mocambique Customs. Jonathan wished he had had a rifle, scopes and a silencer to quieten the creature. It felt again as if the whole world was alerted. For safety, Jonathan decided to take a wide arc around the compound. He couldn't possibly risk being spotted. Every Mocambican was armed and known to be trigger-happy. After all, there was a major civil war taking place in the land. They would cross through the corner of the old mine field which had been laid by the Rhodesians but never cleared. There was however a saving factor. A fire had recently swept through the area and burned all the grass. Blackened root tufts were ideal "stepping stones" offering safety from the wicked mines which would blow off legs or arms, kill instantly or tear up the human body. The team left the road and started hopping from tuft to tuft. Jonathan warned, "whatever you do, don't lose your balance and fall: you could fall directly on a mine! Keep your feet on the root tufts: its' your security - there'll never be a mine where the grass has grown...."

"This is crazy," moaned Babs, now not so sure of herself.

"Fantastic," replied Riga, "I've not done anything like this since my East German days. I love the adrenaline pumping...."

"We're all nuts," put in Pete who was still smarting from his fence escapade.

It seemed that every time the dry burned grass stubs scrunched under their feet alarm bells were ringing in the compound. Every so often, Jonathan stopped to listen and almost seemed to sniff the air for signs of danger. Everything was quiet. Even the mangy dogs had gone back to sleep. The air was crisp but would not stay that way for long. As soon as the African sun poured over the horizon, the temperatures would soar. Time was moving on and so must the team. There was no room for delay. They must be securely under cover before daybreak. Jonathan did not relish the thought of an AK bullet or lounging in a louse infested, flea-ridden prison at the pleasure of the communists.

Jonathan had the distinct idea that his visitors did not quite realize the seriousness nor enormity of what they were doing. This made him feel all the more responsible for them which plunged him back into the military command role he used to play. He whispered orders when necessary, "watch your step..." "don't twist your ankle..." "No whispering..." "don't get behind, Pete." Slowly the team crossed the minefield with Jonathan skillfully weaving a path. He remained "fine-tuned" and in continual comms with the Holy Spirit for direction. It was a life-and-death situation. Finally circuiting the settlement they emerged from the minefield area and breathed a great sigh of relief. Babs and Riga whispered excitedly to break their tension while Pete stood quietly. Jonathan allowed them a breather before leading them to a rocky outcrop where he left them to survey the bush on the opposite side of the road. He moved swiftly across the road disappearing into the bush. Making his way through the thorn scrub he reached thicker vegetation with a few small trees. An old water gully would offer good cover and shade from the heat of the scorching African sun. Having secured the spot in his mind, Jonathan darted back to lead the group to the hideout. It was not far from the main road but far enough for security and would give the team quick and easy access when the vehicles came. By 6.00 a.m. the sun was well up and temperatures were already reaching the 90's. Small flies were incessantly whining around all exposed parts of the body seeking moisture. They'd get into ears, up nostrils, into eyes and even the mouth. Sleep was impossible and the team was quickly devouring the water supply which Jonathan had brought. Riga and Babs were irritated while Pete sat pensively on his own. Without warning, the unbelievable happened. Out of the bush Jonathan caught sight of a native wood cutter wandering nonchalantly along with an ax hanging over his shoulder. His clothes were in tatters and he was unaware of Jonathan or the group but it would not be long before he spotted them. Quickly Jonathan motioned the team to lie flat and crawl swiftly under the overhanging gully. This was war. Behind enemy lines nobody could be trusted. If seen, the man might raise the alarm. Jonathan was quite proud at their sharp, quiet reaction. The man passed by above them without observing anything unusual or even entertaining the slightest suspicion. They all breathed heavily and after awhile emerged like rabbits from a warren.

"Phew," whispered Jonathan, "that was too close for comfort."

"I was praying that he would be blinded," added Babs.

"Thank God," said Riga while Pete merely smiled.

Jonathan thought that quite a response from Pete. Their jubilation was short lived, however. A mere twenty minutes later a second woodcutter appeared. This time he made direct for the gully and couldn't possibly miss the team. As he saw them, he pretended not to see them. Typically Africa. He faltered for a split second before carefully changing his direction, the whole while pretending his eyes had not made contact. He sauntered away but Jonathan knew they'd been seen. This was trouble. He would undoubtedly walk in a great circle until he reached the border to report the incident in the hope of being rewarded. This was how communism operated. Jonathan had visions of truckloads of armed soldiers giving them chase. He was in debate with himself while the rest exclaimed, muttered and bombarded Jonathan with questions. He soon began to give orders. "Pack up, let's move out. We'll go back to the rocky outcrop. From there we can see what happens. It's far enough from the road to give you a great head start if you have to run for it. Let's go!"

They took off, Jonathan scouting ahead. The road was clear and he gave the signal. One at a time the team crossed the road and disappeared among the rocks on the other side. They would gather and then ascend the hill. It was over 100 degrees and the sweat was pouring from each of them but the adrenaline was pumping too hard for anyone to be concerned about the discomforts of the heat or flies. Upon reaching the south side of the road they ascended the small hill and positioned under a large tree well out of sight. Jonathan called Pete,
"You see that tree in the distance?"
"Where?" questioned Pete."Over there, you cannot miss it. The one standing stark and alone. See? That's the border...."
Pete coughed nervously, "I... I... I can't see it. I've a... a left my glasses behind...."
"Oh no, how dumb," chorused Riga and Babs. "Of all the ridiculous things to do...."
"Never mind," cut in Jonathan. "You stay here and I'll get them. Once again Jonathan took off running between the bushes and trees, boulders and gullies. He reached the spot where Pete had laid in the gully and saw his glasses resting on a stone. As he grabbed them, he heard the whine of army trucks. His heart stood still as he hit the ground. "Oh Lord, don't let this be their coming," he whispered. He belly-slid towards the edge of the road to see a convoy - heavily armed - pass by. He waited in the boiling sun. The last truck passed and disappeared around the bend. He waited. His ears strained until he thought they would burst. He listened. No strange noised, no vehicle sounds. In the distance he heard the woodcutters chopping trees. He looked at his watch. It was 9.30 a.m. They had been in place for 4 1/2 hours. Jonathan began to pray that Dick and Trish would come. He had told them to wait in case Jeremiah showed but now he canceled the order in the spirit and sent out a new order. This was an emergency. This was crisis. Jonathan spoke, "Dick and Trish, in the name of Jesus I command you to leave now and come...." Cautiously Jonathan scurried across the road and then ran back to the team. He could tell Pete had really been in trouble from the women. He handed him his glasses and again went through the procedure of pointing out the lone tree and what the team should do.
"If there's any danger you take off with the women and I'll act as a decoy. Don't worry about me. I know this bush and I'll get out.

Just make sure you get across the border there," he pointed, "you'll be safe at that place."

The team collapsed exhausted under the tree. Nobody could talk. All their eyes were closed. Jonathan began to laugh: it was the joy of the Lord....

"It's not funny," interrupted Babs.

"Relax," retorted Jonathan, "God's with us; just be at peace and enjoy it..."

"Enjoy it?" groaned Pete. "This is persecution."

"Listen, listen!" silenced Jonathan, "I'm sure I heard Dick and Trish honking. You get ready but stay here until I give the signal. Two whistles and you come one at a time. Continuous whistling and you take off for the border. Okay? Have you all got it?" Jonathan was quite pleased at the way he was carefully but firmly shaping them into a commando unit. Once again he disappeared. He reached the road and again distinctly heard the sound of the horns. They were coming. They'd received his signal via Holy Ghost frequency. That was true communication and came when believers really submitted themselves to one another and flowed with the Spirit. Jonathan whistled sharply and then again. He considered that Babs would arrive first followed by Pete and then Riga. Jonathan was overjoyed to see the old red Mercedes appear over the hill followed by the pick-up. Both vehicles were towing trailers.

Jonathan stood, waved and then slipped back behind a rock. Caution was still necessary: any army vehicle might be close behind them. Babs emerged from the bush with Pete close on her heels and finally Riga who was having problems with blisters on her feet though she was trying to be discreet about. That determination alone betrayed her. The vehicles had stopped at the spot where Jonathan had strewn stones in the road and one by one the team climbed into the Mercedes. Trish moved into the pick-up to be with Dick while Jonathan took over the Merc. It was a relief to be on the way to another adventure. Trish had had time to share that she had felt an urgency in her spirit at the exact time Jonathan had been praying for them to move immediately. Jeremiah had made no appearance and Dick finally received news that he had caught the bus to Harare. They left without further delay sensing that perhaps something was very wrong. Indeed it had been.

Off they drove, down the road and around the bend and into a roadblock. The team in the Merc were still flustered and excited from their "rescue". There was the first test. "Documenta," demanded the communist captain. Jonathan handed him the passports with that precious stamp. The captain paged through each one silently until he found the stamp. He slowly returned each passport to its owner. There was no smile, no word and certainly nothing friendly. He was finally satisfied and waved on the vehicle.

"Wow," everybody groaned as they moved off. "We made it," they chorused.

"This is going to be a supernatural trip - I feel it in my bones," said Riga.

"Yea, supernatural," parroted Babs. "We're going to have fun."

The team reached Tete by 2.00 p.m. Even for Jonathan who seldom concerned himself with matters of comfort, the heat was oppressive. As usual Jonathan set up camp under the trees along the Zambezi River. Everybody lay around panting and the only slight relief was to completely soak down with a hose and allow the almost instant evaporation to cool the body. Jonathan was in trouble and he knew it. He had had sunstroke before and knew that it was overtaking him from over-exposure. He would be delirious by evening. The afternoon dragged by and Jonathan was drifting in and out of consciousness by sun down. At one point he clearly remembered calling the team to anoint him with oil and pray.

"Agree with me for rain tonight," he muttered. "At least it will cool this air."

"Don't be crazy Jonathan," said Babs. "There's not a cloud anywhere and no sign of rain."

"Just let's believe. He's great." Jonathan prayed while the others added their "amens" more from tradition than any real conviction that God really could bring the rain.

It was 2.00 a.m. when Jonathan was awakened by a strong breeze. He was fully alert. Something supernatural was happening. It seemed God Himself was present. He listened and as he listened he realized he was well: completely healed and delivered from the sunstroke. Suddenly he heard it. It was sweeping up the river. Jonathan just lay and listened in the tremendous excitement of it all. God had heard and a curtain of rain was falling down river and racing up towards them. It was nothing short of a miracle. Every natural indicator was against there being any rain but a supernatural God had intervened in the process of affairs to undertake for His children. If He cares for the sparrows and counts the hairs of our heads how much more concerned is He for our every detail. The team literally lay and soaked up the rain just like the dry parched soil. It rained and rained and rained. Everything was wet but nobody minded in the excitement of the miracle and in the release and comfort which it brought.

Jonathan lifted his voice, "thank you, thank you Lord. What a God You are!"

"I'm taking care," was His reply. Jonathan was very conscious of the presence of the Holy Spirit and knew that the trip was going to be supernatural all the way. Just as the natural rain was poured out, so was the rain of His Spirit going to fall on the team as they traveled. What a blessing, what a reward and what a covering. God's stamp and seal was upon the trip. Of that fact Jonathan was absolutely convinced and what a relief in the face of accusations and slanders from so many quarters that the trip was "not of God" and that Jonathan had been irresponsible for undertaking it and not only jeopardizing the lives of the team but also the very ministry of the church in Zimbabwe. How flesh will always stand in the way of God and the fears and opinions of men quench the drivings and motivations of the Spirit.

"Indeed," he shared later, "God can never take a person further and higher unless there is complete victory at the level at which that person is walking. This is true intercession being lived out. The Spirit has simply got to lead us into deeper truths and revelations: of our weaknesses, corruptions and iniquities, all of which are completely contrary to Him and will always stand in His way of achieving greater things." There was a much greater purpose for Jonathan at that time, of which he knew nothing. But, the Divine Conductor of his life was orchestrating accordingly. What Jonathan did know was that he was standing on TESTING GROUND and he had every intention of passing with high grades.

The morning dawn cool and fresh with slightly overcast skies. "We're leaving for Beira," declared Jonathan though he didn't relish the 450 miles journey with all the roadblocks. The real problem was going to be the checkpoint into the City of Beira, Mocambique's second largest city. It would take another miracle to get into the city especially since the visitors did not have proper documentation. Never had Jonathan entered Beira without being thoroughly searched and investigated. They drove through without incident and as they reached the barrier after the long arduous journey the unbelievable happened right before their eyes. A convoy of army trucks had pulled up in preparation for departing the city limits. The barrier was up and every official and officer was engaged in excited chatter with their departing comrades. Never had Jonathan seen such a thing. "We're going through," he yelled to the team and gave instructions for them to lie flat and pretend to be sleeping. Jonathan gritted his teeth as he looked in the mirror to see what was going to happen with Dick and Trish. They kept on coming: there were no shots, shouts or chases.

"That's totally miraculous," declared Jonathan. "It's never happened before and both vehicles at that. Certainly the Lord is with us. Now we're like Daniel in the Lion's Den. He let us in and He will let us out."

"This is fun," cried Babs. "I'm so excited. Can we swim in the sea?"

"With the Russians yeah," laughed Jonathan. They virtually rule this place. They certainly rape it. Please, please be careful with the camera, Pete. If we once get caught taking photos, it will be the end. Not even on the beach or anywhere in the open must you take photos," cautioned Jonathan. "You'll never know who's a spy or where SNASP might be. It's just not worth the risk. I know it's difficult for you to understand these things but you'll simply have to obey my instructions on this. Usually we put the camera on the dashboard amongst some other things and snap as we drive. There's "no aim" photography in this place - it must all be done from the hip as it were. If you see something just put the camera to the window and snap: it's the only way. Our lives will definitely depend on it. Okay everyone?" questioned Jonathan. "T.I.A., This is Africa," continued Jonathan. I've seen people imprisoned and beaten for the camera crime. We were all detained in Kampala one time just after Idi Amin's rule of terror because somebody didn't listen and took a picture of the airport of all places. I couldn't stop the woman. In seconds armed soldiers ran from every direction and surrounded us with loaded weapons. She lost her expensive camera and after several hours of interrogation we were released minus cameras. It will be worse here as the country's in the midst of civil war."

The team was not staying with Mathilda but with a brother and sister couple whom Jonathan had been teaching and helping. They had been orphaned in the communist take-over and had fought to stay alive. Having only each other Pedro and his sister, Anna made a formidable team who loved the Lord and His saints. They were accustomed to danger and had learned how to make the necessities of life really stretch. They were gracious, hospitable and willing and never complained at their lot. They had quickly learned in the words of Paul how both to abase and abound but being always content, always joyful and always walking in victory. They had been arrested and interrogated several times over the years but they were never afraid and were certainly not hesitant about entertaining Jonathan and the team. They occupied a three-bedroom apartment on the sixth floor. Windows in the block were broken and the elevator had long since ceased to work. It probably had stopped when the Portuguese left. The staircase was dingy and awash with water from some broken pipes. One had to be very careful as the water was mixed with urine and excrement where someone's plumbing had stopped working and the nearest "toilet" was the staircase. It was dark and humid as the team clambered up the stairs to the apartment. At least the cover of darkness made them less conspicuous. Everyone was tired from the long journey so it was not too late before all were ready to retire. Water and electricity were both severely rationed. Every available container was filled with water in the morning and evening including the bath and sinks. There was no hot water. Pedro had rigged up and "Indian" type wash in the toilet since bath always contained water for all purposes. Bathing was to be completed with a half bucket of water. Wet down with a cup; soap down and rinse off. With the humidity it was necessary to bath twice daily - morning and evening. The water was turned on in the morning for only two hours and again in the later afternoon. There was no electricity at all during the day: it was diverted to the industrial sector. In the evening, power was transferred to residential areas and lasted until 7.00 a.m. Of course, there would be days without water or electricity when the anti-communist guerrillas destroyed the power lines.

At 11.00 p.m. a violent shaking of the apartment woke Jonathan from a deep sleep. There was a long low rumbling noise as if an earthquake was stirring the whole city. Flash after flash lit up the night sky so that the whole of Beira was in an eerie type of twilight. Jonathan looked out the window and saw that the docks were on fire. The anti-communist guerrillas had made a hit and scored a "bulls-eye" that night. But everybody was going to pay the price for such blatant boldness.

Next morning, the entire city was swarming with police, army and SNASP. If somebody was not apprehended for the deed, the Governor's head would roll and since he did not intend that to happen anybody was going to be apprehended and immediately tried and sentenced by military tribunal. After all, there was marshal law in the land. Jonathan felt very sorry for the poor unsuspecting Mocambicans. If the Governor was going to be in trouble so too was his entire province. Many would be arrested, imprisoned and shot for crimes against the state. The helicopter and MiGs would scream out and annihilate a couple of villages which would be termed "guerrilla bases" to appease the wrath of the President. Jonathan also began to wonder about their own precarious situation. Every person was having his or her documents searched. The town was "alive" with officials and what with his having "CIA agents" aboard - what a perfect arrest and all okay for the Governor. It would turn him instantly from a "fool" into a "hero" especially seeing that such "spies" were white! What a prize.

While pondering these things in his heart Jonathan began to ask "What shall we do Lord?" The question was not even completed before His reply came simply but profoundly,

"I, who am seated on the heavens shall laugh them to scorn...."

In the simplicity of the reply and the awesome power behind it, Jonathan had the confidence to take on the world.

They proceeded out and for the next ten days the team ministered in the underground churches, swam and lay on the beach with the Russians and traveled around Beira as if they owned the city.

"Well, we did!" declared Jonathan later. "The earth is the Lord's and the fullness thereof and as His children, He was giving us freedom and liberty. We were under His Divine covering and who should dare to interfere with those who were on the King's business?" Not once in the entire time were they stopped, questioned or documents examined. "It was as if God had covered us with a supernatural bubble and nobody could even see us as we moved around. We'd pass right through checks and never get stopped. It was God!" said Jonathan. "He was merely taking care of His own and we became so bold in His confidence."

It was a Sunday evening as they sat in an underground church meeting that the Holy Spirit unmistakably spoke to Jonathan, "pack and leave tonight. Immediately!"

"Are you sure you've heard from God?" questioned Riga.

"It's so late now to leave," offered Babs by way of protest, "We're not prepared...."

The Pastors and believers began to weep and some even fell to the ground grabbing Jonathan by the feet, "You cannot go," they chorused. "It is illegal for somebody to travel at night. The government FRELIMO soldiers will kill you. If they don't, the rebels will get you...."

"And if I don't, God will get me," interrupted Jonathan.

"Oh you can't go. You'll surely die!" they wailed. "We want you to come back!"

Everybody including Dick and Trish were apprehensive about Jonathan's decision and kept up a barrage of questions to see whether he would waiver. After sometime of the doubts and unbelief Jonathan finally burst out,

"That's it! I've had enough. We are going: it's final. Instead of questioning me why don't you ask God? He's not going to tell you anything different from what He's told me."

They said their good-byes to the pastors and drove back to the apartment in silence. It took a couple of hours to collect, pack and tidy the home. Finally everything was in order as they carried their equipment down the stairs. What an incredible time it had been for them: a supernaturally incredible ten days of ministry and fun. Jonathan was not about to let the current climate of things interfere with what God had done even when they reached the vehicles and found the rear tire of the Merc was flat!

"You see," declared Babs, "We're not supposed to depart. There's the warning...."

"This is the devil this time," cut in Jonathan. "He's trying to confuse the issue and stop our departure. Now will you kindly quit that nonsense Babs. We're going and it's final. So leave with us or remain behind...."

The military command shook the team to attention with the realization that it was not a democracy that was in operation and that Jonathan was fully in control. The team settled into their respective places in the two vehicles after having changed the tire. With a prayer and waves at Pedro and Anna who both stood in tears, the two vehicles pulled off. Jonathan was a little nervous. The cordon around Beira would be the testing point. Would they get out of the city? The streets were deserted at that late hour. Very few streetlights were burning mostly because they'd been smashed and never replaced. A cool sea breeze had brought some respite from the heat and humidity making it comfortable to travel. All too quickly they passed the military barracks then the airport and on towards Dondo and the cordon. With rapidity, the spot loomed in front them. Jonathan gasped, "I can't believe it," to the others who were lying flat, "nobody is manning the barrier. Lord, we're going through!" Jonathan tensed as he passed the boom. He braced himself to the first round of shots, the siren or the motorbike chase but nothing happened. Jonathan saw Dick pass through. Nothing happened. Again it seemed as if they were invisible to those around - it was as if God was certainly overshadowing them. "They're through too," cried Jonathan. "We're on our way. Hallelujah!"

Jonathan stepped on the gas pedal and the old diesel Merc began to gather speed. They had a journey of 160 miles with 27 roadblocks. It would take them the best part of the rest of the night to get to the Zimbabwean border and then there was the exit from Mocambique and re-entry into Zimbabwe to be accomplished. There was no time to be wasted. It would be getting light by 4.30 a.m. Any clandestine work would have to be done by an hour before that. In the African summer, natives often rise very early to be in their gardens by first light so as to take maximum advantage of the cool as they work. The team could not possibly risk being seen by a wandering native. They'd already experienced that! If any of the roadblocks decided to search the vehicles they would be stuck for another whole day and nobody relished that thought.

Without warning they were suddenly upon the first roadblock. In the headlights Jonathan saw that the barrier was up. One soldier lay under a blanket near a tree but apart from that nobody else was in sight. After the initial hesitation Jonathan pushed the pedal to the floor and watched for Dick who was following Jonathan's taillights. He kept on coming.

"We're through," shouted Babs gleefully clapping her hands.

"Well Jonathan, it seems you were right after all. I really doubted," confessed Riga reluctantly. That was quite a confession for Riga to make.

The evening was cooling fast as they hummed along. Jonathan thought it would be better if it were raining but then when God is in control what does it matter? It could be broad daylight and they would still sail through. The main purpose of the barriers was to prevent the free movement of the Mocambican population. Under any communist regime, people are rigidly controlled and specifically their movements. They have to carry specially signed passes merely to move from one zone to another within the same district. Inter-provincial movement is a great luxury and privilege for the few.

The next barrier was up and the guard was actually using the weighted handle as a pillow. He stirred as the vehicle passed but made no effort to rise. As they reached each consecutive roadblock it was apparent that the soldiers seemed to have all been drugged. Not one awoke though some stirred. It was the great arched bridge over the Pungwe River however, that concerned Jonathan. He slowed the vehicle as a guard stepped out of the shadows and raised his hand, motioning them to stop. Two things were immediately significant: the soldier had no weapon and was spotlessly clean in an immaculately pressed uniform. In fact, he was regal and totally out of place in the dejected and disheveled FRELIMO communist army.

"Where to?" he questioned Jonathan with warmth and politeness.

"Zimbabwe," was all Jonathan replied as he observed Dick pull up behind him. "We're two vehicles," added Jonathan.

"Proceed," was the only command the officer gave and the "convoy" crossed the bridge. The guards in the middle of the bridge were seated with their backs against the railing. They were fast asleep. On the opposite approach, a group of soldiers sat around a glowing fire. Jonathan couldn't make out if they were sleeping or merely caught up in their own affairs but they crossed the bridge and proceeded on up the road without any hindrances.

"Did you see that?" said Riga. "I'm sure he was an angel."

"Yea," replied Peter with a little excitement in his voice. "This is turning out to be a very supernatural trip...."

"I wonder if he disappeared," cut in Babs. "I'd sure like to go back and see if he's still there."

"I've always been thoroughly searched at that bridge and often by the most unsavory characters. He was so pleasant and had such an authority about him," stated Jonathan.

The Merc was eating up the miles and as the team reached each successive roadblock they encountered the same phenomena: the guards were slumped over in different postures of slumber. Each and every barrier was in a raised position. Nothing was stopping them.

"It was clear," said Jonathan afterwards, "that the angel of the Lord had gone before us and put everyone to sleep and lifted the barriers so that we had a clear passage right through to the border. It was a most incredible journey. There was not a single interruption to our trip and we reached the border in record time."

They stopped the vehicles some distance from the border post. The team was clad in the darkest jeans and while Jonathan gave the order for the rest to remain, he set off once again to scout the entire border and fence. This was not the same border they had entered through and so had to be receded thoroughly. He dashed from shadow to shadow, stopped to listen, circuited buildings checking the most likely places for sentries or watchmen but on the Mocambican side it was totally deserted. Perhaps the angel had passed on through the camp. What God does He does well. The two hundred yards between border posts was open ground. Jonathan crouched as low as he could and darted forward in a zigzagging movement. After fifty or so yards, he hit the ground and lay motionless. He listened. No alarms, no voices, no shots. After sometime the same procedure.

Soon, he reached the tall security fence separating the two borders. As agile as a cat, he moved up and down the fence perimeter checking for mines, wires, booby traps and alarms. There was nothing. Neither were there any guards on the Zimbabwe side. Carefully, Jonathan chose the corner post directly in front of the barracks where he could hear the soldiers snoring. It was open ground but the best possible spot and seemingly the most unlikely but Jonathan felt at real peace. "This is like David's mighty men going to the well of Bethlehem," he mused to himself. "Lord I know you're with us. This had been a spectacular journey!" That reassuring voice which Jonathan had become so dependent upon came in reply,

"I'm here!"

That was enough. Jonathan rather more boldly walked back to the waiting team. Giving last minute instructions to Dick and Trish, Jonathan set off with the rest. He decided to put them through some paces so that by the time they reached the Zimbabwe fence all were breathing heavily and needed to rest.

"Right Pete, you're first. Remember to keep to the pole and swing your leg wide to get over the fence. If anyone gets caught on the wire I will cut them out of their jeans. No noise. As soon as Pete is over, hit the ground and lie still amongst those shrubs. Babs will go next, then Riga and I'll follow last in case there are problems this side."

Pete climbed the fence and with seeming skill and ease moved himself into position and swung his leg over the wire. He dropped silently to the ground. "I bet he's pleased with himself," thought Jonathan. "It was a good effort. . `Hey Babs, tell Pete he did very well. Now you do the same.'" Once again Jonathan thought that Babs who was somewhat stumpy would have difficulty but she ascended the fence and like a skilled climber positioned and swung. She was over and plopped to the ground.

Suddenly Riga began to hesitate and have doubts. Jonathan could not believe that Riga, minus husband would start to hassle at this crucial moment. He cajoled, encouraged, persuaded to no avail. Finally in a stern voice he told her, "Riga you can stay here and get caught then. I cannot believe you're behaving like this. We're in war and others' lives depend on it. Stop being selfish and get moving." Riga moved slowly to the fence in front of Jonathan. They were really compromised and Jonathan knew she was going to bungle the attempt. With her height it should have been easy but Riga put her feet in the wrong positioning. The fence scrunched under her weight as her foot was too far from the corner post and the diamond mesh sagged. The noise was magnified in the still night. Jonathan's imagination began rioting again. He "saw" the barracks alert, lights flash on, soldiers dashing out. Just when he thought she'd made it, Jonathan saw Riga hesitate in the swing and land in the barbed wire. She slipped and hung suspended upside down by the wire. What a noise and furthermore she was about to shriek. Quickly Jonathan instructed her to grab the central upright as he pushed her from below. In a flash he whipped out his knife and slashed her trouser leg free. The sudden realization and fear of being caught spurred Riga into action and in a single move completely on her own, she scaled the fence and dropped to the other side.

Jonathan followed rapidly. Then, leading the team directly under the windows of the sleeping barracks they slipped through the open gate leading to the customs and immigration office and into Zimbabwe. It was slightly past four as they made their way from the border to the agreed rendezvous site. Their relief and excitement, though controlled began to bubble and effervesce.

"What an amazing journey Riga," said Babs.

"One of the best," replied Riga. "Fully up to all they told us about you Jonathan," continued Riga.

"It's been great. Those underground churches were certainly blessed and encouraged," added Pete. "It had been worth it all."

"You know," said Riga, "When a train is moving full force down the track and the driver tries to throw it into reverse, it will derail. I believe that is one thing that God has shown us. This trip was made in heaven and so many people and obstacles tried to throw the whole program into reverse. If they had succeeded we would have been derailed."

The next day after their arrival back in Zimbabwe, the news declared that the Pungwe River Bridge had been blown up by the Rebels thereby cutting off all traffic to and from Beira. "Wow," gasped the team. "They must have done it shortly after we had passed through. Maybe that "angel" kept the rebels at bay for us or maybe he was one of them." Whatever the answer, eternity will tell. In the meantime, if the team had not left that night they would have been detained in Beira and almost assuredly been arrested.

What an awesome God. He made good their escape and went before them to clear a highway just as He had done for Israel when they came out of Egypt. Such experiences of the true living God cannot be compared with anything and no price can buy such dynamic involvement of God in man's affairs.

CHAPTER TWELVE

BLOOD OF THE MARTYRS

The dingy office was a temporary affair with paint peeling off the walls and a somewhat worn and shabby carpet covering the cracked floor. The large oak desk was out-of-place in the worn surroundings as was the large leather chair in which Jonathan reclined surveying the scene.
"It's like the office of a FRELIMO Brigadier," mused Jonathan to himself. "It's incredible that this belongs to a white Pastor in Malawi. I'd rather be out in the jungle in a mud hut surrounded by war than claustrophobic in this musty place." Jonathan was keeping an appointment under sufferance and in true and typically African style, the native Pastor was already thirty minutes overdue. Jonathan knew too, that the inanimate object would be blamed. In Africa it is always "the bus left me," or "the bicycle hit the man," or "the tree was in the road of the car," so that the individual is always with excuse and "innocent." And so, as Jonathan waited, he thought and dreamed.
The last two years had been incredible as the Lord had opened new avenues of ministry. Jonathan's Mocambican role had changed from Urban centers to the vast rural jungles where the majority of the population lived. The long months of prison, the thousands and thousands of miles walked under the most inhospitable climate and conditions, the war scenes of death, destruction and suffering and his own near death all began to pass before his eyes. Despite every adversity, heartache and problem, Jonathan had declared time and again, "the Lord hath buttered my steps." With each new experience and step forward in the ministry and desire to bring the love and beauty of Jesus to suffering, perishing nations Jonathan declared, "I die a thousand deaths and was continuously cast upon that incredible promise of God that I would die in the east of my land. I came to the realization of what death really is: oh, it's so easy to say the `cross,'" declared Jonathan, "but what did it really mean? As I died, I saw that the Holy Spirit was working within to crucify every ambition and desire that is contrary to His nature and

will. Ambition and self was exposed and rooted out. The great concern of the Holy Spirit is with the motives of our hearts and He is continually examining them to replace the corrupt nature of self with the character of Jesus.

Sometime the experiences are distinctly unpalatable but as we allow them to work in us they lend to a greater weight of glory for we are being changed from glory to glory to the image of Christ. That's what it is all about - to be more like Him."

A knock at the door brought Jonathan suddenly to the reality of the moment. Before he could even reply or bring himself back to the present, the door had opened and there stood before him a tall, thin and sinewy African. Actually, the man looked rather gangly and didn't quite know how to carry his height. His dark black hair was Afro style and he wore a rather large pair of spectacles which fitted him very closely.

Jonathan gasped! Never in his wildest imagination could he have anticipated the man who stood before him. He sat upright on the very edge of the chair as he felt the hair on the back of his neck begin to rise and his whole body turn to one enormous goose bump.

With the anointing of the Lord all over him, Jonathan raised his finger to point directly at the man's face with a quivering voice accused, "You're the one. You're the one who did it. You're the one, aren't you?"

The stranger, who was really no stranger, had been transfixed by the amazement on Jonathan's face. Then, it was his turn to be aghast as Jonathan attacked with his accusations. His eyes became large, so large that the whites of the eyeballs were almost glowing. He had a distinctly prominent "Adams apple" which rapidly moved up and down as he kept swallowing, his lips opening and closing like a fish trying to breathe out of water. A thousand pictures, thoughts, ideas flashed through Jonathan's mind as he drove home the arrow with which he had pierced the man in front of him: "Kufa Ufulu, Spirit of Death," said Jonathan mostly to himself but audibly enough for him to hear. "Kufa Ufulu" staggered into the room and collapsed on to a wooden chair near the oak desk.

"H...H...How do you know?' He stammered. "How do you know?" "The Lord has just revealed it," declared Jonathan, "but I think I'd recognize you anywhere. You never used to wear glasses though. How many times did our paths cross?" questioned Jonathan though it was meant to be a statement. Suddenly an incredible wave of

mixed emotions began to well up inside of him: all those war years and there he was, the killer, murderer, destroyer, rapist, satanist: Kufa Ufulu. The Vumba, Elim, Umtali and Wendy all began to shout out accusingly. Suddenly Jonathan knew that he was feeling the same as the early Christians when presented with Paul after his conversion. Large tears welled up from the deepest part of Jonathan's being. He didn't quite know why. Was it for Kufa Ufulu, for victory or the losses or simply in gratitude to God. He was not prepared to analyze as the tears splashed onto the floor. The room was quiet as the man sat slumped in the chair. After a brief interlude, Kufa Ufula let out a long sigh, sat up, looked at Jonathan and said,
"Things have changed now. I'm Garry Mjakachi from Bulawayo, Zimbabwe. I'm saved and filled with the Holy Spirit and I've been to Bible School."
"What?" declared Jonathan. "I want to know all about it. Why did you do it? What possessed you to do such a thing," he questioned although he already knew the answer.
Jonathan had stood up and stepped towards Garry with an outstretched hand of forgiveness and love. They shook hands as Jonathan introduced himself and said, "I'm also from Bulawayo. Salinbornane" in the customary Ndebele greeting.
"I know you and all about you," Garry stopped him short. "I hunted you long enough...."
"Yea, I wish we'd met," interrupted Jonathan laughing.
"I'd have skinned you alive you bugged me so much," retorted Garry.
"I doubt that very much," countered Jonathan. "I had a greater Power than ever you had. You'd have never got me."
They laughed together as they left the room. It seemed so strange calling Ufulu by his real name but there was no doubt in Jonathan's heart that this meeting was ordained in heaven.
"Well Garry, so you're the one who is accompanying me to Nsanje today?" questioned Jonathan. "I have to deliver a consignment of Bibles for the church in Mocambique. We're already late and need to be going...."
"I'm ready Jonathan, let's go."
It was quite amazing how the two "soldiers" became good friends in so short a time and Jonathan marveled at the reconciling power of an almighty God. From hunter and hunted at opposite ends of a spectrum they were united by the Holy Spirit and a love for Jesus

that cemented them together. They bounced along the pot-holed Nsanje Road leaving thick clouds of dust behind the Landcruiser. In the hot October sun the trees themselves seemed to wilt. It was still a good six weeks before the first rains would fall and most people had only just begun preliminary preparation of their fields by burning the grass and old corn stalks. As the 'Cruiser sped along Jonathan looked at Garry and asked,

"Why are you so thin? I'm going to call you `bean pole.'" Garry moved nervously as he laughed. He was full of nervous energy and Jonathan guessed it was from years of living as a terrorist.

"What incredible grace of God: too marvelous and wonderful for comprehension," thought Jonathan...

"Well, what are you doing in Malawi? questioned Jonathan. "Why not Zimbabwe?"

"I kind of wanted to do some evangelism and couldn't settle down in Harare. A friend of mine works with Pastor Sheila and told me she was looking for an African pastor to assist her, so here I am...."

"How long have you been here?" queried Jonathan.

"Oh only a month. But where have you been all this time, Jonathan? I haven't seen you before though I heard from so many Malawians about you. They really do love you..." continued Garry.

"I don't know about that... I travel up and down to Zimbabwe and disappear into the bush for long periods of time preaching and teaching in the villages. I'm not a `town boy,'" said Jonathan. "Shelia often goes out with me. She should know what I do and I'm sure she's told you something. I've been showing her how to be a missionary and teaching her to enlarge herself and her vision...."

"What about Mocambique? Queried Garry who was cut short by Jonathan's abrupt reply, a clear warning not to pry too much about that work.

"What about it?"

"You work there don't you... Er... I mean, you really work inside... a... deep inside."

"Well yes, I walk thousands of miles into the remote areas to preach and take Bibles."

"What about the war?"

"It's hot," said Jonathan "Just like I used to know with you."

Jonathan was deliberately making it tough for Garry. He knew what Garry was after and was going to keep him guessing..

"Well um..." coughed Garry, "Um... how do you a... a manage with um....RENAMO?"

"Oh just fine. They don't bother me," replied Jonathan with a smug grin. He wondered how much Garry really knew. Could he be trusted? After all he had been a top terrorist commander. Did he still work for those who had become the government of Zimbabwe? Years of training had taught Jonathan to be cautious. He was not about to open Hezekiah's treasure house for anyone to take a look. Little known to Jonathan, Sheila was already doing that for him and Garry knew infinitely more than he was revealing. Hence, his searching questions. In fact Garry and Jonathan came to realize after a few years of their relationship had passed that Sheila had, in fact, warned Garry against Jonathan, saying that Jonathan was a spy and Jonathan against Garry saying that Garry was working for the dreaded Central Intelligence Agency which was similar to the secret police operating in many of the Eastern Bloc nations and which had been trained by some of them. It was a divide and rule tactic under which Sheila operated but it did not work in this case as their friendship overcame those barriers she had tried to set up.

With Jonathan's clandestine missionary work in Mocambique it was too risky to say anything at that stage so Jonathan and Garry continued the journey talking about the work in Malawi and the great spiritual needs of the people. It would not take them much more time to reach Nsanje in the early afternoon and they would be camping there that night.

As soon as the vehicle arrived at the village they were surrounded by dozens of children mostly in ragged shorts for boys and torn and faded dresses for the girls. They looked like an army of rag-a-muffins following a pied piper. The boys somersaulted, fell in the dust and rolled over and over or jived in rhythm to some imaginary song while the girls giggled behind their hands. Others played their games of "hop-scotch" much to the annoyance of the boys who felt they were being ignored and who kept interrupting their game. By the time the vehicle stopped amidst the yelling and cavorting children, several pastors emerged from different places. They came smiling and laughing to greet Jonathan and Garry and assist in off-loading Bibles and erecting tents for the night. The "mobile houses" which can be erected and dismantled so easily always fascinate the Africans, from the youngest up. Thus, there was no shortage of willing hands to assist in the operation of setting up camp under a huge wild mango tree which afforded the best shade in the whole area. The temperatures were well over 100 but fortunately there was no humidity. It took very little exertion to cause a soaking sweat and that night with the praise and worship, the heat and numbers would mean that everything would be drenched. There were times when it was so bad that Jonathan had literally wrung sweat from his T-Shirt as if it had just been dropped in water. The natives who were born and raised under the harsh conditions thought nothing of it. And then, of course, there was the mosquito problem. Jonathan rejoiced that there would be very few at that time of the year just before the rains. But, for most of the year they were an incessant army that attacked in droves as soon as the sun dipped behind the Chididi Mountains. Sometimes even the best repellents were not enough to deal with the little creatures. During evening meetings the women would sit with scarves and thrash the air to keep those pests at bay but they always managed to find an arm, ankle or exposed leg. Jeans offered good protection, the material being too tough for their proboscis to penetrate.

The praise and worship lasted a full two hours as the anointing of the Holy Spirit fell upon the people. It was during the harmonious singing of the natives and the blending of their voices that it sounded like the many waters spoken of in the Book of Revelation. Spontaneous cries and the tears pouring down the faces of the unsophisticated villagers confirmed the presence of the Lord who alone can melt hearts like wax before the flame. The anointing was electrifying, so much so that Jonathan wanted to leap straight into heaven. He said afterwards, "I do believe this is what Paul meant when he said `the Spirit... shall quicken' (make dynamic, alive) `your mortal body.' Tragically most believers have never experienced that. It's not emotionalism. It is the living reality of an awesome God touching mortal flesh and giving a taste of a supernatural eternity."

As the singing died down to a period of silent meditation there was such a reality of His presence that Jonathan felt again like doing cartwheels across what little floor space there was. Nobody took any notice of the heat and discomfort because God had come! What anointed, fertile soil into which to sow the seed of His Word. It went forth with power and authority as Garry shared and Jonathan preached. It was past midnight when they crawled into their tents and passed into the restful oblivion of sleep.

Almost a month later after a similar meeting up in the mountains, Jonathan and Garry sat enjoying a cup of tea before retiring. Jonathan was overawed by the beauty and majesty of the heavens as they sat under the stars. There were no mosquitoes to worry about and they could enjoy the magnificence of God's creation without the discomfort of the heat experienced in the valley. Garry suddenly broke the silence.

"Jonathan, how come you've never asked me about it?"

Jonathan paused before replying, "Well I thought you would get round to telling me when you were ready..."

"You're the first one who hasn't pressured me. You know, when I went to Bible School and they found out, I had people visiting me all the time wanting to write my story."

"Well Garry, you really are an example of a trophy of God's grace as was Paul after his `Road to Damascus experience.'"

"I do acknowledge that," replied Garry. "But the thing that really annoyed me is not that they wanted God to receive the glory but they wanted to make money."

Over the next couple of days Garry recounted his incredible story, the contents of which would fill an entire book. Bit by bit, the Holy Spirit pieced together a vast jigsaw puzzle of situations and events which left both men astounded. Jonathan would often say, "Garry, I sure wish I'd met you during the war."

Garry's stock reply became, "I'd have busted your hide," to which Jonathan always laughed,

"I had a greater Power than you my friend and He'd have humbled you. You tried hard enough to get me..."

"Yea," Garry would interrupt, "you so tried me I'd have torn you apart. I actually shot men on account of the fact they let you slip through their hands. Of course now I know why."

"It was light versus dark," said Jonathan "and the Lord would never have allowed you to get me."

"I know Jonathan. I also realize now that I really was a terrorist in a terrorist war."

"Elim! What about Elim?"

"Those people drove us wild. They were so stubborn and just refused to see our point of view. We didn't want them up there in the Vumba. I was area section commander, later to become provincial commander and personally visited the school several times. At first I was a little bit decent but when nothing happened I began to apply pressure by threatening them."

157

"But why butcher them as you did?" questioned Jonathan.

"Well, you see," said Garry, "when I paid a final visit to them I warned them that if they did not move and close the school, we would kill them. I think they had two weeks...."

"And you had agents there all the time. I knew. I even preached there the Sunday before you massacred them. Your men must have attended the meeting. I guess they never reported that it was me."

"What? You were there? Yes, they really slipped up or I would have had you. They reported about some fiery preacher and said they were almost persuaded..."

"Then the preaching was not hot enough." laughed Jonathan.

"Well, I was furious that week when there was no indication from the missionaries...."

"Yes, but they had held a meeting on the Saturday and agreed to move so why did you massacre them?"

"Well," continued Garry, "they never informed me. It was during one evening that we had a wild party. We'd obtained some heroin from across the border and shot ourselves up with it. We smoked dagga (marijuana) all night and drank. Then, in the early hours of the morning we went wild, sacrificing to Mbuya Nahanda and drinking the blood of animals. We also sacrificed a young maiden and it was after drinking her blood that that blood lust took control of us. Those missionaries were an easy target. It was very much like taking the villages: we struck terror into the local people and raped and destroyed and killed. I thought it would be so much better if it were white women.

We rounded up the missionaries that evening and took them to the nearby playing fields. You know it. All of us, we wanted blood: we were savage. The pupils had been given strict instructions to remain in bed and "hear" nothing. What made us so much angrier was that the missionaries said nothing and did nothing. We wanted them to cry and beg but they simply went meekly. We tried to provoke them. Finally, we were so furious that each of us did our own thing. I really don't remember too much more.... I don't... I don't want to say anymore, Jonathan. It's now so painful.

"Well, how did you get saved?" questioned Jonathan.

"Actually in a strange way God must have had His hand upon me. After Elim we moved quickly out of the area to the Sabi. We didn't expect such incredible reaction but Mugabe tried to convince the W.C.C. and others that it was the Rhodesian Army who had done the deed and then blamed us. Of course, we were on the point of death never to reveal the truth. Actually we became heroes and greatly feared for our savagery and daring. After fleeing to Sabi I was crossing an open mealie (corn) field one day when a chopper appeared from nowhere. There was no place for me to hide so I threw down my AK. They had a machine gun pointed at me and the second gunner reached out of the helicopter to grab me and pull me into the hovering machine but such a cloud of dust arose that I couldn't even see the helicopter. I ducked out from underneath it and ran like the wind. By the time the chopper rose up clear of the dust I had reached the safety of the bush and freedom...."

"Wow, what an escape, Garry."

"Yea! The second escape was more incredible. One day I was actually captured with a friend and tied up. That particular night they assigned two coloreds (mulattoes) to guard over us. We began to talk to the doods and finally convinced them that after winning the war they would be heroes and well rewarded if they helped us... Fools! When we reached our camp we whipped those men every day for a week just to make sure they were genuine...."

"Incredible," whistled Jonathan, "What savagery."

"Well, we knew if they were genuine they would stay no matter what their treatment. We took no nonsense from anyone. It was part of our security."

"But how did you get saved?" insisted Jonathan.

"It was the end of the fighting when we were all grouped into the guerrilla camps awaiting the outcome of the elections. We had very little to do and life was somewhat boring. We troubled the local people, raped the women and forced the villagers to brew beer for us. I ended up in a camp in Matabeleland. I'd spent most of the war in the Eastern part of the country but now at the end wanted to be nearer home in the south. Anyway, one day I received the newspaper, the Bulawayo Chronicle. As I paged through it I saw this crazy advertisement entitled 'CALLING ALL COMRADES,' followed by the testimony of some woman named Margaret. Before that, we'd often enjoyed terrorizing believers. We'd march into a church on Sunday night and while the pastor was preaching we'd walk up to him and draw our pistols holding them to his head and threatening to blow his brains out if the congregation didn't leave. You never saw such a stampede as people fled. It was always hilarious to us to see all those church goers behave in such a cowardly way. It made me realize they didn't really believe in what they were doing because they weren't ready enough to die for it."

"You do have a point there, Garry. But you know, there are some people who can't be bought and sold or compromise because of fear," lectured Jonathan. "Continue anyway."

"Well, we'd literally roll on the ground laughing at those weak people. Some of those pastors actually wet themselves with fear. We thought it was more fun than terrorizing villagers. We decided to just get hold of this Margaret and we'd deal with her the same way and see how tough she was. There was a Bulawayo address so I wrote her telling her we'd seen the advert and wanted to know all about `this Jesus.' I had grown up in a Christian home, Jonathan. In fact, my father was a pastor in the Assemblies of God so I really knew all about it...."

"And your day of reckoning was coming!"

"It certainly was and quicker than I knew," continued Garry. "You see, we had no intention of hearing about Jesus. We intended to get this Margaret out to our camp where we'd rape her, kill her and then feed her body to the crocodiles. It was common procedure for those we termed `undesirables.'

The completed letter I carefully placed in the pocket of my camouflage trousers and buttoned up that pocket. As we drove to the post office I was quite excited about the thought of the treatment we were going to give this Margaret. But the most incredible thing happened."

"What? What?" questioned Jonathan.

"When I reached the post office the letter was gone. Clean gone, I tell you. I searched everywhere but I know that I had put that letter in my pocket and it had vanished. I was, myself, instantly terrified. I knew the supernatural well. I could sense it and smell it and the disappearance of that letter was supernatural. I thought immediately that the ancestral spirits were displeased with me and were coming to get me. I suddenly felt drained of all my power. My legs and arms had no strength. I collapsed and my men had to carry me back to my Landover. I don't know how I managed to get to my room where I fell on my bed shaking and sweating. The men thought I had contracted a sudden bout of malaria but I knew it was far more serious. Bodyguards surrounded me day and night. They were to protect me but failing that they were to kill me as I had so much information and knowledge that I couldn't possibly be allowed to be questioned by anyone. As soon as I was on my bed those bodyguards settled down to a game of cards while I went through incredible torment. I don't know how long it lasted - maybe an hour or so - when suddenly the guards started shouting. Chairs toppled over, men fell on the floor while some fled the room. I was petrified at seeing the horror on some of the men's faces. I leapt from the bed even though still incredibly weak and as I swung around there on the wall was a circle of light with a flaming cross in the middle. I couldn't move. Suddenly a hand, the hand of God descended into the room. In His hand appeared blocks, like wooden blocks and He began to thrust them into my open mouth, block by block. I realized that on each block there was writing, it was scripture verses. As the Word was entering my mouth I saw like a vision and the demons were leaving from my feet. I had dozens of them. They left screaming and fighting but they had no power to stay and I had no power to do anything. Resistance from either was out of the question. God was fully in control and there was to be no more arguing with Him.

After sometime I was completely free. I felt as if I was floating on air though I was very weak after the ordeal. I wept and wept you know, just like a baby and I just couldn't stop myself. The next morning I went out for early morning parade. Usually if my men did anything wrong I'd severely punish them. Torture and punishment was my game. But that morning as I went to shout at the men, all that came out of my mouth was 'Praise the Lord.' The entire parade ground came to a complete halt and gazed at me in absolute astonishment. They couldn't believe their ears. Now you know."

Garry excused himself and went to bed while Jonathan sat and pondered the mightiness of God an His unfathomable love and grace. Knowing Garry and the type of terrorist he had been made Jonathan marvel all the more at how God had preserved him for a greater purpose and plan which He had already begun to reveal.

A couple of days later after a stirring meeting, Jonathan and Garry sat down to a traditional village meal. Small cakes or patties of white, steaming corn meal lay in one plate while the "relish" or soup lay in another. The relish that day was half a small chicken in a very thick, salty, tomato broth. Lumps of meal were rolled in the fingers, dipped the broth and swallowed with a gulp and much smacking of lips. (The corn or maize, called "ncema" in Malawi is seldom ever chewed. The thick salty relish is neutralized by the very starchy ncema). As they swallowed their "dough balls" as

Jonathan called them, Garry picked up his account. He said "Jonathan you make all this look so easy, the teaching, preaching and praying."

"Actually it is Garry - when you trust Him. I had to die to self and still am. One thing I remember was God telling me He'd have to undo all I had done at university. That's kind of humbling. By the way, how long have you been saved now?... Oh, of course, five years. How long were you at college?"

"Three years, Jonathan. But before that I had a long learning process. I corresponded regularly with Margaret and we had become good friends. She worked at the main Police station in Bulawayo and did so much to encourage and teach me many basics. Of course my first and biggest problem was after the elections because I just did not want to be part of the Party anymore, or the army, or the government. My uncle is a minister...."

"Well, you do have influential friends Garry...."

"They mean nothing now, Jonathan. I just want to serve the Lord."

"So, how did you get away from the 'system?'"

"Oh, I don't think I have. You see, I was brought before all the hot shots and powers-that-be. I was quite renowned during the war...."

"Yea, I sure knew you and wanted you badly."

"And I you, my friend. Anyway, I told the Party leaders that I just wanted to go to Bible School and serve the Lord. They were furious and tried to persuade me this way and that but my mind was made up. They didn't understand and thought I'd gone crazy."

"So, what happened?" questioned Jonathan.

"Finally they agreed to give me sometime to `think it over,' hoping I would `see reason'"

"Is any of them saved?"

"Oh definitely not. That's why they thought I'd gone mad. After all the fighting and then it came time for the spoils and I was not interested. They couldn't understand and giving me time to think it over wasn't going to change anything. Eventually they reluctantly released me and told me to `go to my school,' but even now, I know I'm not free. They'll never let me go especially knowing what I know.

"So you're still in danger?"

"Yes, Jonathan. They often sent somebody to spy on me and have tried to associate me with overseas spy organizations. You know that is their favorite trick. But enough of that. Of the group who were involved in the Elim Massacre, two were killed in a car crash while the rest, including myself, all attended Bible School and are in the ministry today.

"That's wild! That's God! It's no wonder those guys are furious with you and think you've taken leave of your senses, Garry," agreed Jonathan.

"The greatest problem I faced was from fellow Christians and friends. You know everybody believed I was working for the government, that my life had really not changed and I was sent as a spy!"

"Ha! Ha! Ha!" laughed Jonathan. "I've been there and know exactly what you mean."

"What do you know about that?" queried Garry.

"It's a long story, I'll tell you one day." Jonathan was not quite ready to take Garry into his fullest confidence especially with the warning from Sheila still warm in his ears. On the other hand, he had learned that Garry was genuine, talented and aggressive - characteristics which made Sheila jealous. She was aiming to make mileage out of Garry's preaching abilities and popularity. Jonathan knew that that often happened in the ministry because people do not know their callings and feel insecure. He, himself, had often experienced those type of reactions against him and felt somewhat protective towards Garry for that reason.

"So many people tried to get me to write or dictate the story for them and I had quite a turbulent time at Bible School. One person even came armed with a pistol. You know..."

"What? That's unbelievable Garry. What did he want to do?"

"I'm not sure but it was my first experience of a Word of Knowledge. God showed me he had the weapon. I overpowered him, took it away and held it to his head...."

"That old nature boiled up strong eh?"

"Oh boy, in my old days I wouldn't have hesitated to pull the trigger. Instead I warned him to clear out with his dirt and tell all others that they would get it if they harassed me anymore. That largely brought an end to my troubles."

"And you finished Bible School in peace?"

"More or less," added Garry.

"And so here you are in Malawi,"

"Yea it's incredible meeting you..."

""It's God my friend."

At other times Garry shared with Jonathan how he'd fled from home and caught the train that morning. How he realized now that he had been running from God for all those years and had tried to fill the emptiness with his friend the AK 47. He shared how on his travels for training he had met people like Tito and Castro. "That was historic for me then, Jonathan. I'd achieved my dream. I was something and these men were my heroes. Of course I was deceived but I didn't know it at that time. Now of course, Christ is my hero."

Jonathan and Garry became firm friends. Jonathan in fact, came to love Garry and enjoyed working with him though he was always restless and insecure. Few understood the real pressure under which he operated and the system which seemed to have tentacles always trying to suck him back and enslave him. Time and again the men would share their experiences during the seasons when they had been on opposing sides.

"Jonathan, I was so mad when you missed that mine in Maranke. I heard those two whites radio for you. That's why I didn't kill them. Actually, we came right up to them. They begged us not to... You know, I hated anyone who begged me."

"I wouldn't have begged," said Jonathan.

"Yeah, I guess not; you'd have fought back. By the way Jonathan, what did happen that night when we attacked your base. We trained all our firepower on your cottage.... I was so desperate to wipe you out."

"So it was you. Incredible!"

"We saw you go down. How did we miss?"

"Oh, it was an angel, Garry."

"Come on, tell me another."

"No, I really saw him and after that I just knew I wouldn't die."

"The Lord must really love you," was all Garry said.

It was four months later that Garry planned a routine trip back to Zimbabwe to visit his family. He disappeared. Seven years later, on a preaching tour of England, Jonathan met with, of all people, Margaret in a town near Bristol. In passing conversation, Jonathan made mention of Garry, not even knowing the connection at that time.

"Oh," she said, "I know Garry."

"You mean that Garry? questioned Jonathan in surprise.

"The one and only - the same," replied Margaret.

"From where?"

"Well, I was the one who really directed his salvation."
"Amazing! What on earth's happened to him? asked Jonathan.
"Do you ever hear from him or know where he is?"
"Oh yes, he's living and preaching in Birmingham. I have his 'phone number and address."
A few days later Jonathan and Garry renewed their friendship and Garry shared of his escape from Zimbabwe six years previously.
"I went to see the leadership," declared Garry. "I was so sick and tired of being followed. I told them to leave me alone and get their thugs off my back."
"That was pretty daring, Garry."
"I was just tired of those doods. They never left me alone. All I wanted was to mind my own business. Why couldn't they understand that? I never interfered with them."
"Maybe they were frightened you would tell or write all that you knew," proffered Jonathan.
"My parents are there, Jonathan and my family. You know how it works. They bought my silence but it's never enough."
"So then what happened?"
"Well they told me to come back that afternoon and they would give me an answer."
"Weren't you afraid?"
"Of course, but my life had become a living hell anyway so there was nothing to lose. I tell you, it was tough. I sure paid for all that I had done. Hmmm," uttered Garry as he pondered some thoughts.
"And what did they say when you went back?"
"They told me, "Okay Garry, you are free. We will release you today but never speak of the war or you know - the other thing, or else you will be in trouble."
"Thank you," I replied and backed out of the office. As I turned to say good-bye, the Holy Spirit clearly spoke and told me not to trust a single word and to leave the country immediately.
"That very night," continued Garry, "Some armed henchmen came for me at my sister's apartment. It was only by God's grace that I managed to give them the slip and I fled to Bulawayo and then on to Botswana. That's how I ended up here. "Incredible,"
Jonathan whistled, "so you are a fugitive then!"
"Yeah Jonathan, but I plan to visit my parents next year. I'll fly to Botswana and walk into Zimbabwe like the old days. Actually you know, I've been seriously thinking of getting involved in the political field."

"Ah Garry, forget about all that. Concentrate on the Gospel. That's the call the Lord has placed upon you. Come back to Africa and work with me. You're an African and the Continent needs you. Aren't you tired of running?"

Jonathan and Garry discussed late into the night and Jonathan ended by pleading with Garry, "Please, please don't visit your family until there's a change. They'll get you. You're too well known."

Garry simply laughed his usual choking-type laugh and said, "Okay my friend." The last time Jonathan and Garry met was for a few days fellowship in London prior to Jonathan's departure. His last words to Garry were, "Promise me friend, you won't visit home!"

Garry laughed again but never made the promise. We heard that he disappeared there in 1993. Heaven alone knows all the answers!

CHAPTER THIRTEEN

NEW BEGINNINGS

The Book of Acts, which sets the tone, methodology and momentum for the Church of the New Testament, portrays the history and achievements of some very ordinary men and women who were recklessly abandoned to the will and purposes of God.

"It is a simple matter," says Jonathan, "to not only believe in the bigness of a big GOD but to obey Him. There is no unknown dimension with God, because he is the God of the UNKNOWN. All that is required is for us to step out on the water and walk with Jesus. It is a wonderfully diverse and exciting life and when we launch out beyond the realm of our own comfort, security and knowledge is when God will take us into the spectacular. Great grace was upon the early Church and this led to notable miracles. Our same God is ready to pour out great grace again and again. The problem is, we have become a results oriented society, which has lost dignity and honor in favor of achievement. The most important thing of all is that we grow to be more like Him and allow His beauty, compassion, dignity and purity to shine in a darkened and perverted world."

Experience - personal encounters - of the Lord and with Him brings an intimacy and friendship into the relationship. "I believe this to be one of the most absent things in the Christian life today," says Jonathan. "And, it is for this reason that the majority of God's people live and walk a shallow Christian life. But, it doesn't have to be that way at all. The church is standing on the very brink of eternity and as Daniel the prophet declared, 'they who know their God shall be mighty and do exploits.' There has never been such an opportunity in ecclesiastical history as today when men can do great and mighty things for Jesus and the only limits are those that we impose upon God and ourselves by our very unbelief. There remains over 11,000 unreached people groups in the 'Valley of Decision,' who need missionaries to put in the sickle and harvest."

Jonathan's story of being "Recklessly Abandoned" is the account of an ordinary person who believed and obeyed his extraordinary

God. "Recklessly Abandoned" is a true account of only some of the major highlights and a preparation for even greater things which took place in Mocambique and are recalled in the sequel "Love Constrained."

Just as God delivered the Hebrew boys from the furnace, so He is well able to deliver from bullets, bombs and mines. The Bible reveals that they went everywhere preaching and teaching with signs following and this is Jonathan's expectation. The Body of Christ is going to return to this type of living reality so that miracles and healing and deliverances will no longer be spectacular but will be every day occurrences. In the Africa of Jonathan, it is not spectacular for somebody to raise the dead and when such miracles take place in the jungles there are no videos to explode the event into fame and undermine the servant and the gift. The reason that the book has been long in coming is because of Holy Spirit restraint. But the Church with all of its gifts, talents and incredible resources is going to have to learn how to live dangerously in the days ahead. There is coming incredible persecution upon the whole earth: a persecution far worse than communism and the only way to overcome is to love dangerously, give dangerously and live dangerously.

All of his experiences prepared Jonathan for some of his toughest living, which lay ahead, and the continued "death" of which the Lord had spoken. Jonathan continually spoke of being up where the eagle flies: above the turmoil of the world. "People are searching for the kingdom of God but it is within us," he said. "The tragedy is that the church has gone full circle to the position held by the disciples shortly BEFORE Pentecost. They wanted to know about the restoration of the Kingdom of Israel. Today so many believers want their material empires while whole nations are searching for the TRUTH. The government is upon His shoulders and because it is upon His shoulders it is upon ours. Once we know the Truth and Government of Almighty God, we are absolutely free: freed from the opinions of men. The promise which God made to Israel was that wherever they placed the soles of their feet it was given to them and I believe the same applies today,' declared Jonathan. "I don't have to own any physical territory for the meek have already inherited the whole earth. Indeed the meek are they who delight in the Lord and the abundance of His peace. Once that delighting takes place, there explodes a peace that translates you into a new dimension with the

Lord: a place in the Spirit the same as that which the eagle attains in the natural. Paul indeed speaks in Romans that the kingdom is not meat and drink. We are so concerned with these things. We have such abundance but still are never satisfied. I've seen natives in the jungles barter gold for salt and give their last morsel of food to me with delight and joy. How moving and humbling that has been. No beloved, the Kingdom is righteousness and peace and joy in the Holy Ghost. Now we are righteous in Him and so I believe the righteousness of which He speaks are those personal encounters which enflame our lives afresh and anew. The abundance of peace comes in delighting in Him whom our soul loves and we, because we have his fullness, have everything and our job is full. That's true authority and rulership. The affairs of this world cannot affect you; you are above them because you are in Him. I have learned how to both abound and be abased but in all things to be content. That's freedom."

There is no doubt that intercession is a major factor in the enlargement of a servant of God. Prayer and intercession are keys in Jonathan's life which keep that intimacy with the Lord. Those who will dare to live "Recklessly Abandoned" will experience similar encounters especially as the forces of darkness are unleashed upon the earth. It will become a matter of habit to be transported as was Jesus and Phillip and others. It will be common to be fed by an unceasing flow of natural provisions from supernatural sources as was the widow of Zarephath. It will be expected that prisons built for believers will be shaken and angels lead the captives free. It is time to trust in God and not our resources or abilities. God enlarges the individual step by step. Just as soon as we have gained a new position or level with the Lord is as soon as He places some new obstacle or task before us so that we can grow further in grace. It is just like climbing a ladder rung by rung. We can never comprehend the unfathomable riches of God's love towards mankind and with one willing vessel, He is able to do abundantly above the highest expectations of men.

Jonathan became a willing vessel to preach the Gospel to unreached areas. Despite the ravages of war: the death, destruction and pillaging, he never allowed those things to interfere with God's moving upon his heart. The cry of mostly Third World natives with all the complexities, poverties, sicknesses and diseases attracted Jonathan because they had attracted the Holy Spirit. The knowledge of the glory of the Lord shall fill all the earth as the waters cover the sea. "It is not so much preaching the Gospel - that's the easy part," Jonathan declared, "but it is daily living before the natives and showing them that there is a more excellent way. It's not a western way. I will never concede that I am trying to impose a western way upon them because I'm not. But, I believe that my own lifestyle has become more and more married to that of Christ so that it is a Biblical life-style."

The western missionary has suffered untold abuse from Third World natives who continually make the accusation they are being forced to westernize. Jonathan himself is an African in an African world, knowing their cultures, their fears, the power of witchcraft and the family system. It is from these that Christ has come to set men free. That freedom does not come because people hear a Gospel message. It comes because servants are willing to make themselves of no reputation and die to live in the darkness and show that more excellent way. Show that you can live in the midst of withchcraft and not bewitched or die because the power of Christ is greater than satan's. Show that hard work, discipline and commitment will lead to prosperity and blessings. Show that it is more blessed to give than to receive. Show that the Gospel works practically in day-to-day living if men will but obey its requirements.

"There is no such thing as short-term missions," says Jonathan. The very idea of `missionary' is one who is sent out. Home becomes the place where the will of God is operating. Neither do I believe that it should be left to national leaders to evangelize their own peoples. There are no limits, borders or barriers with God. While the Third World definitely needs the expertise and teaching of the First World, it can certainly show the latter the zeal and anointing which once it had."

If only the billions of dollars spent each year on ministries flitting around the world was given to true missionary endeavor, what incredible inroads would be made. Jonathan is ready to make such new inroads because there burns in his heart a love for the lost and continual stirrings of the Spirit which prompt him yet on to greater heights. There are always new beginnings in God because He's not only a God of restoration but of enlargement. The destiny of an entire nation was changed because of that obedience to God. May He alone receive all the glory and honor, dominion and power.

OTHER BOOKS BY MICHAEL HOWARD

LOVE CONSTRAINTED is the sequel to "Recklessly Abandoned" about missions work in war-torn Mocambique and how God used ordinary people to change the destiny of a nation through intercession

THE ONLY GOOD ONE IS A DEAD ONE is real stories of African snakes and how alike they are in character to the devil. An unusual look at breaking soul ties.

THE PRICE OF DISOBEDIENCE is a study on the price paid by a person, church or nation when they do not obey God's mandate for them.

WHAT IS YOUR DESTINY is a powerful exhortation to the Body of Christ today to line up with the Word of God and carry out His plan for your lives as individuals, as a Body and as a nation.

THE PERVERTED GOSPEL is an end-time book which reveals how the Body has taken different aspects of the Word and made them into Gospels thus perverting the ONLY GOSPEL.

TALES OF AN AFRICAN INTERCESSOR is a new look at intercession which will inspire and change your life and encourage you to be intercessors - the only thing that will see the Body through in these last days.

PROVEN ARROWS OF INTERCESSION is a handbook which lays out principles of intercession. Intercession is a discipline in relationship and has everything to do with knowing the heart of the Father.

THIS IS THAT is a booklet of stories compiled by W.E.C. from letters sent home to England from missionaries who experienced a tremendous outpouring and revival in the Congo in the early '50's.

SERMON ON THE MOUNT is a powerful book and takes a look in detail at each of the aspects of Christ's Sermon of Matthew and how they should become part of every believer's life.

FEASTING AT THE KING'S TABLE is a timely book on Holy Communion and our need to celebrate on a regular basis.

CONTACTS

SHEKINAH MINISTRIES
P.O. Box 34685
Kansas City, MO 64116 USA
Tel (816) 734-0493
Fax (816) 734-0218
Email Shekmin@aol.com

SHEKINAH MINISTRIES
P.O. Box 186, Station "A"
Etobicoke M9C 1C0
Canada
Tel (416) 626-1543

SHEKINAH MINISTRIES
17 Wayside
Weston-super-Mare BS22 9BL
England
Tel 011-44-1934-629785
Email: mark@mwinterton.fsnet.co.uk

SHEKINAH MINISTRIES
Evajarventie 178
35400 Langelmaki
Finland
Tel 011-358-400-903535
Email: daisyhome@dlc.fi

KALIBU MINISTRIES
P.O. Box 1473
Blantyre, Malawi, Africa
011-265-633187

Email Kalibu@malawi.net

KALIBU MINISTRIES
P.O. Box 124
Escourt 3310,
South Africa
Tel 011-27-363-525399

KALIBU MINISTRIES
P.O. Box 55
Banket
Zimbabwe
011-263-67-26293
Email: jeanf@icon.co.zw